SHERLOCK MYSTER... ...I...

VOLUME 4 NUMBER I   July/August 2013

FEATURES

FICTION

CLASSIC REPRINT

ART & CARTOONS

Publisher: John Betancourt
Editor: Marvin Kaye
Assistant Editors: Steve Coupe, Sam Cooper

Sherlock Holmes Mystery Magazine is published by Wildside Press, LLC. Single copies: $10.00 + $3.00 postage. U.S. subscriptions: $39.95 (postage paid) for the next 4 issues in the U.S.A., from: Wildside Press LLC, Subscription Dept. 9710 Traville Gateway Dr., #234; Rockville MD 20850. International subscriptions: see our web site at www.wildsidemagazines.com. Available as an ebook through all major ebook etailers, or our web site, www.wildsidemagazines.com.

FROM WATSON'S SCRAPBOOK

So here we are in our ninth issue of Sherlock Holmes Mystery Magazine. I confess to some trepidation that it would not last this long, though Holmes never had any doubts whatever, and that I do believe is a function of his ego—new adventures of the illustrious detective? Why, how could anyone resist?

In the following pages, you will encounter perhaps for the first time my account of that unpleasant business of The Five Orange Pips. I have also given permission to Mr Jack Grochot to interpret my handwritten notes (no easy task, for what they say about a physician's cuneiform is, alas, true) of The Case of Vamberry the Wine Merchant, which I declare to be one of Holmes's more impressive performances, as well as a go-ahead to Mr Bruce Kilstein, a fellow physician, to tell the dramatic recounting of The Blackheath Collapse.

At first, Holmes was somewhat reluctant to permit this periodical to be published, but he is now an enthusiastic supporter thereof, for he feels that he has been handsomely and accurately represented in these pages. As for myself, I am always and ever pleased to receive royalties for my efforts.

Holmes and I both look forward to the next issue, which shall consist solely of his ratiocinative exploits. Indeed, it will contain The Field Bazaar, which was not a case at all, but instead, a domestic scene between Holmes and me at 221B.

But now I must report on a new publishing venture that fills me and Holmes with chagrin. Some ragtag rascals who call themselves publishers intend to print new versions of some of my tales about Holmes with the added element of erotica perverting the plots. We have tried to secure an injunction against this disgusting effort, but because of some legal loophole we cannot do so. This, by the way, is not the first time this sort of thing has been tried. I have in my library a blue (literally as well) pamphlet which had me relating how I treated the wounds inflicted on the villain's wife in The Hound of the Baskervilles. Said injuries required my rubbing in ointment ever so gently to her aching naked buttocks. Of course, this never happened, but it was at least rather mild and its tone was as gentlemanly as possible, so I chose to ignore its existence. I doubt, though, that such good taste will be evident in the upcoming publications.

Now I shall turn over this forum to my colleague and co-editor, Mr Kaye.

— John H Watson, MD

Welcome back! It is always a pleasure to edit this long-overdue magazine that celebrates the many adventures of Mr. Holmes and Dr. Watson, as well as other tales of crime and mystery.

In addition to the three aforementioned Holmesian adventures, our contents this number includes stories by Marc Bilgrey, Carla Coupe, Jay Carey, John M. Floyd, Paullette Goudet, Janice Law, and Nijo Philip. I was especially taken by the nastiness of Ms. Coupe's all-too-real villain—actually, it was not he who I was glad to read about, but his altogether deserved punishment. I also quite liked Mr. Floyd's charming tale, Valentine's Day, about a new elderly distaff detective. We will be publishing more of her adventures.

The upcoming tenth issue of *Sherlock Holmes Mystery Magazine* will, as Dr Watson said, be entirely devoted to Holmesian stories. Among its participants will be Carole Buggé, Peter Cannon, Herschel Cozine, Christian Endres, Jack Grochot, Martin Rosenstock, Mark Wardecker, and Zack Wentz. The nonfiction section will include a study of Sherlock Holmes and science-fiction (!).

—Marvin Kaye
New York City
March, 2013

COMING NEXT TIME ...

It's another special
ALL SHERLOCK HOLMES FICTION ISSUE!

Sherlock Holmes Mystery Magazine #10
is just a few months away...watch for it!

SCREEN OF THE CRIME

by Lenny Picker

MILLER TIME? HOW TV REINVENTED HOLMES FOR MODERN TIMES—AGAIN

It took me nine episodes for the new CBS drama *Elementary* to win me over. I had watched an advance copy of the pilot with my long-suffering wife (regular readers of this column, if any, may recall that she endured screening multiple versions of *Hound*, and one-is-more-than-enough viewing of *Sherlock Holmes and the Deadly Necklace*—watch this space for details of that experience), and we both found it enjoyable enough. But with memories of the mind-blowing second season of BBC's *Sherlock* fresh in our minds, this version of a Holmes walking modern streets, using 21st century technology, felt less than compelling.

I dutifully recorded the subsequent episodes on my DVR, where they sat in a virtual pile of unwatched programs. Eventually, my schedule cleared a bit, and I made my way through episodes two through eight, without much changing from my initial impression. There were too many parallels with USA Network's *Monk*—an eccentric sleuth, a female "companion" attempting to keep him in line, a friend on the force with a younger police colleague. And

Benedict Cumberbatch and Martin Freeman cast a huge shadow, and will likely do so for some time.

But the series, from the outset, did carve out a unique niche in the large universe of screen adaptations of the Canon. No, not in having a female Watson (or the functional equivalent)—there was Joanne Woodward in 1971's *They Might Be Giants*, Jenny O'Hara opposite Larry Hagman's Holmes in 1976's *The Return of the World's Greatest Detective*, Margaret Colin in 1987's *The Return of Sherlock Holmes*, and Debrah Farentino in 1993's *Sherlock Holmes Returns*. (By the way, all of these were in contemporary settings.) And not in the New York City setting—apart from *They Might Be Giants*, who could forget Roger Moore and Patrick Macnee in 1976's *Sherlock Holmes in New York*, not that some of us don't wish to?

So what is really novel here (there is something new under the sun), is the emphasis placed on Holmes's addiction to narcotics. It is that destructive habit that led his father to hire Joan Watson (Lucy Liu) as his sober companion, and gave this Holmes (Jonny Lee Miller) a foil to help him get through the initial transition after a stint in rehab. (The setup makes it less than surprising that Watson's role in Holmes's life continues well past the time of her original engagement.) Thus, it only makes sense for Holmes's former drug use, and struggle to avoid relapsing, to be part of every episode. We see Holmes at meetings of fellow addicts, watch Watson attempt to hook him up with a sponsor, and her fear that he's gone back to drugs when he drops out of sight.

In an experience of Holmes on screen that extends over four decades and two continents, I am not aware of any series that puts this problematic aspect of the character front-and-center. (The film of *The Seven Percent Solution* obviously did so on the big screen, but about midway through, Freud helped Holmes kick the habit, making the action-packed denouement indistinguishable from other films; and had Nicholas Meyer's superior—and less ambitious—second pastiche, *The West End Horror*, made it to film, that picture would not have.) And it is a problematic aspect; with my 12-year-old sons about to delve into the Canon, how do I explain my attachment to and reverence for a character who abuses his body on a regular basis? And given Holmes's love of logic, how could he not absorb the reasoned arguments Watson made about the dangers of cocaine and morphine: "Count the cost! Your brain may, as you say, be roused and excited, but it is a pathological and morbid process, which involves increased tissue-change and may at last leave a permanent weakness. You know, too, what a black reaction comes upon you. Surely the game is hardly worth the candle. Why should you, for a mere passing pleasure, risk the loss of those great powers with which you have been endowed?" (*The Sign of the Four*). If guessing was destructive to the logical faculty, as Holmes stated in *The Sign of the Four*, how much more so was the introduction of mind- and mood-altering chemicals?

Small wonder that adapters have treaded lightly here; the Rathbone *Hound* ended, illogically, with him calling for Watson to get him "the needle." The Canon rationalizes the use of drugs as a coping mechanism to deal with boredom, and as a substitute for mental stimulation—circumstances that didn't apply when he'd just laid the Baskerville family curse low. That throwaway line, which was literally thrown away—cut from initial prints of the film—adds less than zero to the plot or character, and it's as close as the Rathbone series got to acknowledging Holmes's addiction.

Something about adapting *Hound* brings this out—the 2002 Roxburgh version has Holmes shooting up in the midst of the case, which is even sillier, given that the Canonical Holmes justifies his use of cocaine, by stating that he would resort to "artificial stimulants" only in the absence of strenuous mental exercise from a challenging investigation.

But clearly, focusing on Holmes as a recovering addict is not an out-of-left-field gratuitous addition to the character. And the problem is handled naturally; at the outset, Holmes does not share his recovery with his liaison with the NYPD, Inspector Gregson, fearing that it will disqualify him from serving as a consultant to the Department. And Watson is explained away as a valet or personal assistant.

Having Watson hired by a thus-far-unseen father to Holmes (as opposed to a more canonical paternal elder brother Mycroft) is also an interesting innovation. Show co-creator Robert Doherty commented on this aspect of *Elementary*. I suppose that it humanizes him in certain ways.

Holmes wasn't "made," he wasn't sent here from space—he's a real man with a real family from a real home. There are stories to tell about how he got here from there, why he does what he does, how he got along with his family, etc. I look forward to meeting Dad one of these days.

And humanizing Holmes, in my view, is essential for viewer engagement. If the Holmes of the books, or on radio or the screen, was actually "the most perfect reasoning and observing machine that the world has seen," the character would not be so popular over 125 years after his debut in print.

Miller's Holmes is less acerbic than Cumberbatch's, and more sentimental. That is best-illustrated by the ending of episode nine, "You Do It To Yourself." The main plotline centers on the murder of a professor (a puzzle inspired by one of the canonical tales), but the subplot is just as gripping; Watson is contacted by Liam Danow, her former lover, who is also a heroin addict. This back-story fleshes out the character nicely and results in a very moving closing scene (nonspoiler alert—it has nothing to do with the murder mystery).

Watson thinks that Liam may finally be ready to get clean permanently and arranges to meet with him at a clinic. Given their shared history, and her understanding of the challenges of addiction, her presence at the appointed time is a triumph of hope over experience.

To her surprise, and the viewer's, Holmes shows up to keep her company; he knows that Liam is a likely no-show, and rather than let his friend go through the anxiety of waiting alone and going through the shattering disappointment when lingering no longer makes any sense without support, he's there for her. They sit quietly, as the mournful, downbeat lyrics of No's "The Long Haul" (no, I never heard of this band, either, before) play. It's a powerful ending, and a moving one, that made me want to rethink my attitude towards the series.

Miller is not Cumberbatch or Brett or Merrison or Rathbone. But, with *Elementary* green-lit for a second season based on its high ratings, at the end of that season in 2014, Miller will have played the part in over 40 episodes, almost 29 hours (in these diluted days of 42-minute hour dramas), which would elevate him to the very first rank of portrayers of the Master. (I haven't done the math on the Ellie Norwood silent films, but Clive Merrison's radio Holmes aside, only Jeremy Brett's 45 episodes will rank ahead of

Miller, a distinction that a third season will shatter). And in terms of viewership, only Robert Downey, Jr. is in the same class.

So for many, Miller's Holmes will be the Holmes they first experienced. Having his Canon-derived flaws out in the open and an integral part of the portrayal may not be such a bad thing, even if the format of the show dictates less complicated cases, and less brilliant deduction than BBC's *Sherlock* showcases. The concept may have originated when Doherty and friend Carl Beverly (now coexecutive producer for the show), started kicking around Beverly's idea of "Sherlock Holmes in New York City."

But in choosing to highlight something that was background at best before, the pair have hit on an interesting new interpretation.

✗　✗　✗　✗

Lenny Picker, who also writes for *Publishers Weekly*, can be reached at chthompson@jtsa.edu.

ASK MRS HUDSON

Dear Mrs Hudson,

I wonder what the most dangerous case might be that Mr Holmes personally involved you in? I am guessing it may be the one Dr Watson called "His Last Bow," although he did not personally narrate it. Details would be appreciated!

Sincerely,

Lillian Prendergast
Montclair, NJ

✗   ✗   ✗   ✗

Dear Mrs (or Miss) Prendergast,

Thank you so much for your missive—it is much appreciated, and does my heart good to know someone is reading my little literary efforts, such as they are. I would not presume to intrude upon Dr Watson's territory—he is the true writer—but I am always gratified to hear from my readers.

Actually, the most dangerous case I was personally involved did not so much contain risk to myself as it did Dr Watson. In fact, I think the dear man was so disturbed by what happened that he never put pen to paper to write about it. I have on two occasions mentioned it to him, but when I do, he goes quite pale and makes some excuse or other as to why he is too busy to write about it. I am not possessed of his literary gifts, but I will do my best to narrate it in brief here. It was in the early days of Mr Holmes and Dr Watson's tenancy, and I daresay if it had happened later the outcome would have been different.

The story concerns a Miss Valerie Carstairs, who arrived at Baker Street on a wet afternoon in late October. She seemed most distressed, and when I escorted her upstairs, Dr Watson greeted her and invited her to sit by the fire and tell him the purpose of her visit. Mr Holmes was out, engaged by Detective Lestrade in a case of grand larceny that he later said was quite easily solved—but as he was not to return for some time, Dr Watson persuaded the young lady to tell her tale to him. As I was serving them tea, I chanced to hear the main points of it myself.

It seems the young lady's former fiancé had taken it rather hard when she broke off their engagement, and continued to plague her with repeated letters, visits, and most recently, threats to her person. You can imagine Dr Watson's reaction to this—ever the gallant protector of women, he fairly seethed with rage and determination to send this young blackguard on his way. Though I begged him to wait for Mr Holmes's return, he insisted that this case called for no keen deductive powers, but rather the kind of stalwart fortitude that he as a former military man could offer.

The young lady's insistence that her fiancé (whose name was Edmund Simpson) was a dangerous man fell on deaf ears—Dr Watson's sense of chivalry had been aroused, and he insisted on calling upon the young man immediately to warn him to cease his harassment of Miss Carstairs. Perhaps sensing the good doctor's intentions, Simpson refused to see him, even though he was clearly at home when Dr Watson called. I was persuaded to call upon him myself later than afternoon, on the pretext that I was a long-lost aunt who had come into some money that I wished to leave to him. What ambitious young man can resist such an intriguing suggestion, even if he suspects trickery?

I was duly admitted into the household, while Dr Watson waited out of sight—and just before the door closed behind me, he forced his way into the establishment and confronted the miscreant in his foyer. While Miss Carstairs had informed us the young man was dangerous, she failed to mention that he was a fencing champion—or that he kept a collection of swords in his foyer. Grabbing a well-sharpened foil, Simpson attacked Dr Watson while I watched, horrified. The poor man received several nasty wounds before my screams brought help in the form of a constable whose daily beat luckily took him past the townhouse in question.

Mr Simpson was arrested and charged with assault and attempted murder, for which he received a lengthy prison term—the jury being moved by the introduction of his repeated threats to Miss Carstairs into evidence.

Dr Watson recovered from his wounds, though the slash on his shoulder left a scar and continued to ache in damp weather. I think his pride was injured as well, as he never spoke of the incident afterwards, and, as I said, has refused to write about it. Mr Holmes has never brought it up since, knowing, I think, how it pains Dr Watson to think of it. After that he seldom went on a dangerous case with Mr Holmes without bringing his service revolver.

There is another very dangerous case that I was personally involved in—a bit too personally, perhaps, and if you care to read it, you may do so in the novel The Star of India, which has been recently rereleased by Titan Books.

Thank you again for your interest.

Most sincerely,

Martha Hudson

✗　✗　✗　✗

My dear Mrs Hudson,

I am a professional chef at the Harwichport (MA) Inn. I have thoroughly enjoyed the recipes you include from time to time in your columns… especially the Tuna Varenka, which I have served to our customers to great success.

I wonder two things… first, whether you trained as a cook in your younger days, and if so, where? And secondly, might you suggest another good seafood recipe, which we would like to place on our menu and name it after you, if that idea does not displease you?

With culinary greetings,

Joseph T. Lavinson

✗　✗　✗　✗

Dear Mr. Lavinson,

You do me honour with your compliments, and I thank you humbly for your kindness. I feel unworthy of such praise from one such as yourself—a professional chef, upon my word—but thank you for your generous comments.

In fact, my aunt was married to a Frenchman, and though I received no formal training, I spent many a happy hour at her side, learning the secrets of French cuisine, such as the difference between a béchamel and a veloute sauce, how to make a soufflé rise (the secret is in the whipping of the egg whites, as well as a pinch of cream of tartar), and the creation of duxelles, that heavenly mixture of mushrooms, shallots, onions, and herbs in butter, which figures so prominently in Beef Wellington. (I find wild mushrooms have more flavour than cultivated ones, if you can get them.) I say with some pride that Mr Holmes and Dr Watson have always enjoyed my own version of that classic dish, though I don't suppose they know I learned it from my aunt. Mr Holmes, while always courteous, seldom inquires about my personal life unless he thinks it may have relevance to a case he is working on.

English cuisine, such as it is, can be a hearty but plain affair, which is why my childhood experiences with my aunt have stood me in good stead in satisfying and hopefully pleasing my tenants, the longest (and most dear) of which is of course Mr Holmes. I humbly offer another of my recipes for your enjoyment, Hudson Sole (since you suggested naming it after me.) Such a delicate and tender fish requires a more subtle treatment than mackerel or cod, I think, so this recipe is designed to coax out its natural, refined flavour. This is a recipe Dr Watson is especially fond of, and I usually make it with fresh Dover Sole.

Very truly yours,
Martha Hudson

✗　✗　✗　✗

HUDSON SOLE

Four fresh sole fillets
Butter, 4 oz.
Fresh Cream, 6 oz.
Shallots, 2 large
Cream Sherry, 6 oz.
Fresh parsley, one bunch, coarsely chopped

Sauté shallots and set aside. Place sole, butter, cream and sherry in baking dish; sprinkle with shallots and half of the parsley. Bake at 350 degrees for approximately 20-30 minutes, checking after 20 to see if fish is done. Do Not Overcook. Remove from oven when done and sprinkle with the rest of the parsley. Serves Four.

✗

"The coroner suspects Humpty-Dumpty may have been pushed!"

BONEYARD

by Marc Bilgrey

Dave laughed as he pulled Rachael by the hand through the dark cemetery. They stopped for a minute under a tree to catch their breath; as they did, Rachael looked up at the moon. In that instant, a bat swooped by.

"I'm not sure this was such a good idea," said Rachael.

"You're not scared, are you?" Dave asked.

"Maybe just a little," said Rachael.

Dave surveyed the area, then pointed to a spot about two hundred feet from where they were standing. "There," he said, "that's where we'll do it. Right between those two big gravestones."

"Maybe we should go back to the car."

"Don't be ridiculous, you're the one that always said you wanted to do it in a cemetery."

"Saying it and actually doing it are two different things."

Dave squeezed Rachael's hand and led her to the place he had pointed to. "Well," he said, "let's get down to business."

"How about a little romance?"

"This isn't about romance, it's about lust and the thrill of doing it in public."

"This place gives me the creeps."

"Of course it does," said Dave, "it's a graveyard."

Rachael stepped over to the large headstone and read the name, Smith. "Oh, great," she said, "well have the whole family watching us."

"Nobody's watching us, they're all dead." Dave sighed. "You're taking all the spontaneity out of it."

Rachael turned to Dave. "You said this would put some spice back in our sex life, but now that we're here I..."

"Forget it," said Dave, "just forget it."

Rachael glanced at the moon and said, "I want to go home."

"So go home," said Dave, both disappointed and angry. "What are you going to do now?"

"I don't know."

"You're not going to stay here."

"Why not?" said Dave, feeling more angry by the second. "This is where our marriage belongs. These dead people have as much of a sex life as we do."

"Go to hell," said Rachael, walking away.

"If I was in hell at least I'd be getting laid."

Dave watched Rachael disappear over a hill. A few minutes later he heard a car pull away. *I try to liven up our marriage*, thought Dave, as he began walking, *and this is the thanks I get*.

Dave wondered if he should stay at a motel in the area or call a friend when he got back to the city. By the time he reached the bottom of the hill he was already feeling better.

That's when he saw the woman in the black dress. She had shoulder length blond hair, high cheekbones, red lipstick, and a shiny string of pearls around her neck.

"Hello," said Dave, as she approached.

"Hi," she said, "I don't usually see anyone here at this hour."

"Do you work here?" Dave asked.

"No, I was just visiting my husband's grave. I come here sometimes, at night, it's quiet. My name's Linda."

"I'm Dave. If you don't mind me asking, how long ago did your—"

"He died twenty years ago."

"You must have really loved him."

"He was much older than me. I respected him a lot. What about you?"

"Uh," said Dave, "I was just sort of looking for someplace peaceful to do some thinking."

"It doesn't get more peaceful than this," said Linda, as she gestured to a stone bench that was part of a nearby grave site. "Come sit down and talk to me."

Dave sat down, smelling Linda's perfume. It had the scent of honeysuckle.

Linda asked Dave about himself. He told her about his marriage and the lack of love he'd been feeling for the last couple of years. A few minutes later, Linda took Dave's hand in hers and gently kissed him on the cheek, and then on the lips. Soon they were on the grass, making love. Afterwards, they held each other.

"Where do you live, Linda?" asked Dave.

"My home is here," she replied.

"What do you mean?"

"I'm Linda Smith, you were looking at my gravestone before."

"No," said Dave, "seriously."

Linda sat up and looked off into the distance. Her eyes widened. "It's my husband," she said, "and he's coming this way."

"But you said your husband is dead."

"Exactly."

Dave turned to see a figure standing at the top of the hill, silhouetted in the moonlight.

"Linda!" yelled the man. "You miserable slut! You better be alone or I won't be responsible for the consequences!"

Dave ran across the cemetery toward the main gate, but, as he approached it, three men in dark suits stepped out from behind trees and blocked his path. Dave turned to go back in the direction that he'd come from, when he saw Linda walking toward him.

"They don't look too happy," said Linda.

"Who are they?" Dave asked.

"I was married to all of them."

"I don't understand."

"It was a few years before your time, Dave," she said. "They called me the Black Widow, though they could never prove a thing. That's because I always used a different method, arsenic on one, sleeping pills on the other…"

"How am I going to get out of here?" Dave asked.

He felt Linda's soft fingers touch his shoulder. "What's your hurry, Dave? I'm really starting to grow very fond of you…"

✗

BULLY FOR YOU

by Carla Coupe

I hate bullies. Always have, always will. They're one of the few things that can distract me as I work.

I pegged Frank DeMezzo as a bully the minute I set eyes on him. He looked like a Hollywood actor—one you'd see testifying before Congress about human suffering, or holding the hand of a frail child in a TV commercial. But the bully seeped from his pores, flashed in his eyes as he brushed past me in the hall, sending the stack of thankfully empty lunch trays I carried clattering to the floor.

"Watch it." He threw the words over his shoulder, like litter from a car window. Sparing me a glance, he wiped his hands on a handkerchief, smoothed his well-cut jacket, then entered his mother's room.

Brooke, another "housekeeper"—we were glorified maids, really—dashed down the hall to help. "It wasn't your fault, Sarah," she muttered. "That Frank is a piece of work. How such a nice woman could have such a jerk for a son …."

Later, I passed the open door to Maria DeMezzo's room and glanced inside. Frank sat in the one comfortable chair, facing the window that overlooked Sunny Meadow Nursing Home's soft, green lawn, bordered with daffodils and tulips. A woman's voice quavered a question.

Frank's "don't be ridiculous, Mother," echoed down the hall. "We discussed this last week, and you agreed I was right …."

Yes, I hate bullies. And Frank DeMezzo topped my list.

"Thank you, Sarah. That's much more comfortable." Soft-spoken and graceful, Mrs. DeMezzo leaned back in her bed. Frank obviously inherited his good looks from her. I tucked the wool blanket in at the foot, smoothed the lacy coverlet.

A bang at the open door, metal on wood. "Maria? Did you tell Frank about the money?"

Maria's eyes fluttered shut for a second and she released a small sigh. "Hello, Annabelle. No, I haven't."

The metal walker banged against the door frame again. Annabelle Quince shuffled in, her salt-and-pepper hair pulled back in a bun, her fuzzy black cardigan buttoned to her chin. The cardigan snagged on the door lock, leaving behind a clump of black fluff. She gave me the once-over. "So you're the new girl."

Girl. At forty-three. Not because I was young by comparison with the inhabitants of Sunny Meadows. No, because I was a maid. I bit my tongue, held my temper in check. I couldn't afford to lose this job. Not yet.

"Yes, ma'am. I'm Sarah Reilly."

Annabelle looked at the bed, then at me. "You're just as careless as the last one. Listen, girl. For the amount my no-good son's paying to keep me here, I want a nice, smooth bed, too."

Mrs. DeMezzo frowned, a crease appearing between her arched eyebrows. "Now, Annabelle. Sarah is new, but I'm certain she did an excellent job."

I'd just made up Annabelle's bed, taking care that it was every bit as smooth as Mrs. DeMezzo's, but I kept my voice soft, my eyes down. "I'll remake your bed as soon as I finish here, Mrs. Quince."

"I'll be checking up on you." She hobbled around the low, well-padded club chair to the wing chair in the corner and groaned as she eased herself onto the high seat. "I'm telling you, Maria, if you don't stop giving that boy money, he'll end up draining you dry."

I closed the curtains, shutting out the twilight that deepened into night. Frank took money from his mother? Didn't surprise me. In the bathroom, I refolded the towels and wiped the sink and toilet seat. Both showed evidence that Frank had used them. A blind man had better aim.

"It's difficult for him." Mrs. DeMezzo sounded worried. "The banks are being unreasonable, and he can't expand the business without—"

"Business!" Annabelle barked a laugh. "I don't care what he tells you, he's not using it for business. Look at those suits! And his car. You said he just moved into a bigger house, with a pool and media room, whatever that is. He's spending money like water."

"He's my only child. I can't disappoint him."

"Listen to me, Maria. I know how to deal with children. If you don't say 'no' now, he'll take you for everything you've got, and you'll end up in some rat-infested home with…" She paused. "Cockroaches."

"Cockroaches?" I could hear the loathing in Maria's voice. Annabelle certainly knew Mrs. DeMezzo's buttons.

"And fleas."

I slipped out of the room, grabbing the fluff trapped in the lock. Annabelle was as much a pig as Frank.

"**M**other! You can't be serious!" Frank's shout carried down the hall to the tiny closet we used as our housekeeping room. "You promised me that fifty thou—" A door slammed, cutting him off.

Brooke handed me a stack of towels from the cart and grinned. "That's a first. I guess Frankie won't be able to buy himself another new sports car with Mom's money."

"A new sports car? Must be nice to have such a generous mother."

She laughed. "Well, I wouldn't know. But Mrs. D.'s always given Frank whatever he wants. Wonder why she's grown a backbone now."

I didn't wonder. Brooke and I walked down the hall together, and even through the closed door we could hear Frank's muffled shouts.

I frowned. "He sounds pretty upset. You think we should look in on Mrs. DeMezzo?"

"Feel free." Brooke checked her watch. "I'm taking the rest of these towels to the south wing, then I'm on break."

A familiar metallic thump drew our attention. Annabelle stood in the hall, banging her walker against Mrs. DeMezzo's door. "Maria!" she bellowed. The other residents would complain; even deaf old Mr. Rangely at the end of the hall could hear that.

Brooke rolled her eyes. "See you later."

"Maria!"

I hurried toward Annabelle. "Is something wrong?"

"Don't be stupid, girl." Annabelle banged the door again. "Open this damned door."

I juggled the towels into one arm and swung open the door.

Frank's voice cut off again.

Annabelle clattered through the doorway, her cardigan catching on the knob. A wad of fluff drifted to the floor. "Afternoon, Maria, Frank. Just thought I'd drop by for a visit."

I tidied up the fluff and peeked into the room. Frank, his back to the window, scowled at Annabelle. Mrs. DeMezzo sat in the wing chair, her head bowed, her hands folded in her lap. The sunlight picked out the veins beneath her thin, pale skin.

Frank pasted on a smile, but his tone was frosty. "Good afternoon, Mrs. Quince. If you'll excuse us, my mother and I are—"

"Oh, don't mind me." Annabelle stumped over to the club chair and settled herself with a grunt. "Your mother and I don't have secrets."

Frank's smile thawed and broadened. "Then you can convince her to help her only son. It's a short-term loan, designed to—"

"Forget it." Annabelle sniffed. "I told Maria not to give you a cent. She's going to end up in the poor house if she keeps financing your freeloading ways."

Frank stared. "You told her to …." His face reddened. "Why you interfering, lying bit—"

"Frank!" Mrs. DeMezzo gripped the chair arms. "How could you use such language to a…a friend!"

"But Mother," he turned to her, leaned down and covered her hand with his, "she's ly— not telling the truth. Your comfort is important to me."

Annabelle snorted, and Frank glared. He turned back to his mother. "You know I wouldn't ask, except—"

"No, Frank." Mrs. DeMezzo raised her chin. "Annabelle's right. I'm not going to lend you any more money."

"But Mother—"

"I can't afford it." She shook her head, bit her lip. "I know it's hard for you, Frank, but—"

"Don't weaken, Maria." Annabelle leaned forward, eyes sparkling. "You don't want to get kicked out of here."

Clenching his fists, Frank took a step toward Annabelle. "You're responsible for this. By God, you'll regret interfering with me."

He whirled and barged through the door. I stepped away, but he knocked me aside, sending towels flying. Staggering, I grabbed his jacket. The pocket tore.

With a curse, he pushed me away. I stumbled into the wall.

I watched him stride down the hall and round the corner. After straightening my uniform, I knelt and began gathering up the towels.

"Hear anything interesting?" Annabelle stood in the door, grinning.

I flinched. I'd been so absorbed in my thoughts, I hadn't heard her coming.

She jerked her head at the towels scattered across the floor. "That'll teach you to sneak around and listen at doors."

"I wasn't—"

"Don't lie, girl. You're as bad at lying as Frank is."

"But Frank threatened you, ma'am." I looked up at her. "Aren't you worried?"

"Him?" She laughed. "Frank talks big, but he's a coward. Maria never taught him right. I beat respect into my boy, and I'd have done the same to Frank." Annabelle waited until I collected all the towels, then crossed the hall to her room. "You made a mess of the bed again. Come back after my nap and do it properly."

She closed the door behind her.

I managed to remake Annabelle's bed between cleaning rooms and collecting laundry. Tighten the sheets, smooth the pillows. Annabelle wouldn't find fault this time.

After my break, I passed the reception desk. Cindy waved me over and pointed to a basket filled with red and white carnations and greenery. "Sarah, would you take these to Mrs. DeMezzo?"

"Sure. Who're they from?" The carnation petals drooped, the greenery edged with brown.

"Her son dropped them by, but didn't stay." Cindy curled her lip. "Typical cheapskate. Carnations instead of roses, and this arrangement's so old it's ready for the trash."

In the hall outside Mrs. DeMezzo's room, Brooke carried a dress on a hanger, covered with a dry cleaning bag. She frowned at the dress. "I hope Mrs. Quince is happy this time. I think she's sent her dress back three times so far."

"She wouldn't be happy with these." I lifted the basket of flowers.

"Frank's peace offering." Brooke grimaced. "It'll be lucky to last another day."

Mrs. DeMezzo's room was empty. I checked to make sure the flowers had enough water, then placed them on the side table. She would see them as soon as she entered. When I came out, Brooke was closing Annabelle's door behind her.

She looked startled. "Oh! I thought you'd gone to the laundry."

I trailed her down the hall. "Guess she liked the dry cleaning job."

She grinned over her shoulder. "Don't know. She was asleep."

"That's odd." I hurried to catch up. "She had a nap earlier."

"Maybe she's not feeling well." Brooke didn't sound concerned.

"Should we check on her? Or tell one of the nurses?"

Brooke stopped and turned. "Listen, Sarah. You're new. If Annabelle Quince decides to take a second nap, or even sleep all day, that's her business. The best thing to do is leave her be."

I took Brooke's advice.

Mrs. DeMezzo's scream brought everyone running, even Mr. Rangely, who hadn't heard a sound in five years. We clustered around Annabelle's door. I couldn't see much in the dimness, just Mrs. DeMezzo weeping by the window. Annabelle lay still on the bed. Murmurs of "strangled," and "quite cold" passed from person to person, like a chill December wind.

Finally Doctor Pitman pushed his way through the crowd, telling everyone to move away. I helped settle several of the residents, promising to let them know what had happened as soon as I found out.

Mrs. DeMezzo's door was open, and I peered in. She sat in a chair, her eyes red but dry. Brooke stood behind her, patting her clumsily on the shoulders.

"Can I bring you some tea or coffee?" I spoke softly, even though it wasn't necessary. Annabelle certainly wouldn't care.

"That would be lovely." Mrs. DeMezzo touched my arm. "Would you stay, dear? I'm sure Brooke wouldn't mind bringing me a cup of tea."

"Sure." Brooke looked relieved as she left.

I gave Mrs. DeMezzo a cool, damp washcloth for her eyes, then sat beside her and held her hand.

Brooke appeared with tea and the news that the police had arrived. A tall, lanky detective spoke with Mrs. DeMezzo first, then asked to talk with me.

We met in the airless room usually reserved for grieving families. "Yes, sir?" I perched on the edge of a big leather chair. The detective seemed almost bored by my answers to his questions, until he asked if Annabelle had any enemies.

"Enemies? Like someone who threatened her?"

He perked up. "Did someone threaten her?"

I paused, staring at my hands folded in my lap. "Frank DeMezzo was very upset with Mrs. Quince, but I'm sure he didn't mean anything by it."

The detective cleared his throat. "We'll be the judge of that."

After the detective dismissed me, I returned to Mrs. DeMezzo.

She dabbed her eyes. "I can't stop thinking about her. Annabelle."

"Would you like to talk about it?" I asked.

Her smile wobbled at the corners, but she nodded. "I wanted to thank Annabelle for encouraging me to …. Well, to make certain decisions that would ensure I could stay here."

"That's when you found her?"

"Yes." She squeezed my hand. "It was horrible. Her face was discolored, and there was something white around her neck …."

A handkerchief. Yes, I knew.

The phone rang, and I handed her the receiver.

"At the police station? Oh, Frank!" Two tears rolled down her cheeks. "Don't answer any more questions until you have a lawyer, Frank. I'll call Drew Waverly."

She listened for a moment, then frowned. "No, I won't be able to pay the retainer. You'll have to find the money somehow. Maybe you could mortgage your house, or cash in some of your investments." Her tears stopped.

I closed the curtains. It looked as if Frank would be charged for the murder of Annabelle Quince. Earlier, I had overheard the detectives talking about the monogrammed handkerchief—initials FDM—used to strangle Annabelle, and a wad of fluff from her cardigan found in Frank's jacket pocket. One that was torn, as if in a struggle.

Poor Mrs. DeMezzo. She'd been through so much. After she phoned her lawyer, I persuaded her to take the sleeping pills the doctor had left, and waited with her until she drifted off.

I missed my usual bus, but the administrator offered to pay our cab fare home this one time. I asked the cabbie to stop at the shopping center a couple blocks away. Outside the all-night drugstore, I fed money into the pay phone. Two rings before I heard, "Well?"

"Your mother's gone, Mr. Quince."

A loud sigh. "Excellent."

"I know these things are always a relief."

"Yes, indeed. So you'll be on your way, then?"

"I'll quit when the police finish their investigation."

"Police? Wait a minute! You told me it would look natural."

"I changed my mind. Don't forget, I'm the pro. I seized the opportunity. And I had the perfect fall guy: another bully."

A dry laugh. "Poetic justice, eh?"

"Yes." I grinned. "Two bullies for the price of one."

✗

THE HEREAFTER PARTY

by Paullette Gaudet

It was the smallest of ads, in the most disreputable of newspapers, so of course it caught my eye: "HAD ENOUGH? Need help ending it all? Spend your last days with us."

I carried the torn newspaper listing in my wallet for two weeks before calling the German agency and submitting to their questionnaire. I wrote a check, and received a map with directions. A business concern brought me to Germany soon afterward, and I used the map to arrive at 38 Rhineland Strasse.

Apartment B-5 was the number I was directed to buzz, so I buzzed it. A clipped, British voice directed me to come up, so up I came. Thirty steps brought me from the busy German street below to a dingy wooden door with a tarnished brass B and 5 on it. The door was unlocked, and inside amidst richly colored floorlamps and velvet upholstered chairs stood a short, middle-aged man with a tight moustache and bowler hat. His plump frame was rather dashingly camouflaged by a brushed flannel suit of deep blue, which complemented the more piercing hue of his eyes.

"Rafferty, yes?" he asked.

"Yes," I replied.

"Splendid! Have a seat!"

And so I sat, to listen to the plan of my impending demise.

I am not a melancholy sort, by nature. It had just become all too much, as it were. There were financial failures that might possibly have been fixed, and familial distress that could most likely have been resolved. All in all mine was not the worst situation ever seen, but for the past six months I had considered myself the sorriest creature in the world, one whose obliteration might afford some monetary comfort to my nearest and dearest. I had considered the available options, and decided not to pursue them. I wanted to die, but at the very least wished to die well. That is why I was at the Braeburn-Drury agency.

"Tea?" Mr. Braeburn asked, from under his bowler hat.

"Please," I answered.

"We have your contract typed up, but wish to confirm the details with you. You are, as of now, listed under 'Quick and Painless,' is that correct?"

"Yes, I believe that is what I specified."

"We are wondering if you'd like to broaden that definition. To 'Slow and Tortuous,' perhaps?"

I blinked.

Mr. Braeburn chuckled. "Heavens, no, what good would that do anyone? What I mean to say is that death, by nature, is a solitary event. However, one can ostensibly use one's death to further a greater good, creating a non-living legacy, as it were."

"I don't quite follow."

"Say, for example, there is another's death you might wish for. We might combine your suicide with that, thereby killing—well, you know the proverb."

"Are you suggesting I become some sort of suicide bomber?"

"We're thinking more along the lines of your own personal enjoyment, in those last moments of life. Something you've never done, for fear of death. Something you've never considered, for fear of retribution. Going out with a bang, so to speak. Living through dying, and all that."

Mr. Braeburn's words made perfect sense, on the one hand. I had never walked barefoot on the beach, for fear of hookworms. I had never taken a gentleman's holiday in Thailand, for fear of incriminating Internet photos. I had lived in a narrow box, fearful of death and humiliation, and now had the opportunity to truly taste life before severing all ties to humanity.

"Go on," I said, and crossed my legs.

"More tea?" Mr. Braeburn asked. I nodded as he laid three documents before me.

"The answers to your questionnaire noted the perceived attentions of a Mr. Percy Ambrose toward your wife, correct?"

"Yes," I said. Percy Ambrose was an accountant fifteen years my junior who frequented my London townhome for financial appointments with my wife, Corbella.

"Relations between you and Corbella have not been good as of late, have they?"

Corbella's auburn curls and creamy skin were but a distant tactile memory, having been untouched by me for twenty-seven weeks. "Relations have been strained," I allowed.

"Mr. Ambrose has also recently made adjustments to your investment portfolio without your knowledge or consent."

"Corbella attends to our financial affairs, she was schooled for that. I trusted that her meetings with Mr. Ambrose were for the mutual benefit of our marriage."

"Hm. It appears that her settlement in the event of divorce has been increased, and that the paperwork for this required only one, fifteen-minute meeting."

"Corbella has seen Ambrose at our house every Tuesday at 2 o'clock for eight weeks."

"Yes. But aside from a slight shift in investments and the divorce settlement, there have been no other changes to your financial affairs."

"Then why…would so many meetings be needed?"

Mr. Braeburn removed his bowler hat and traced its rim with his thumbs. "Here at Braeburn-Drury we deal only in facts, and leave imagination to our clients."

I placed my teacup in its saucer with a resounding rattle. "I believe I am ready to die."

"Splendid! Your signature is required on two more forms, then we can begin."

How do you wish to die? was the first typed question on the Braeburn-Drury questionnaire I received in the mail. I had imagined several possibilities, none of them suitable. I could lie on a silk-sheeted bed, knocked to a corpse by prescription painkillers. There were the messy options of guns and razors, or the leap off a building. There was the slow death of cancer, brought on by smoke and drink. But, I had already spent hours in pubs, habitually taken two sleeping pills above the recommended dosage, and had a fear of heights that threatened to asphyxiate me at the thought of changing a lightbulb. If I was going to die, I wanted to do so with some semblance of nobility. I wished it to be an event that my children could sob about into the arms of future, sympathetic collegiate lovers: "My father…died while attempting to thwart a bank robbery, and/or assassination attempt, or by pulling nuns from a burning building." That would satisfy the basic requirement of me being dead, and theirs of having a brave parent to be proud of. Corbella would most likely not care how I died, what with being busy in the arms of Percy Ambrose.

I had left my Essay of Desired Death blank—had chosen the "To Be Announced" option. I could not come up with a death I deemed grand enough to suit my life, and decided to entrust strangers with that burden. My own scenarios were too plebeian, too sniveling. I needed guidance for greatness in death, and for that looked to Mr. Braeburn in his bowler hat.

"Your questionnaire states that you enjoy driving motorcars," Mr. Braeburn said.

"I do like a quick turn on country roads at dusk," I confirmed.

"You also spend a fair amount of recreational time playing home video games, particularly those involving the accruement of points by running over property and pedestrians."

I shifted in my chair. "My son's game, the only one in the house."

Mr. Braeburn gazed at me with unblinking blue eyes. "Have you ever run over anything, anything at all, on these twilight motor excursions of yours?"

An inappropriate sting of tears met my eyelashes. "There was a squirrel, once, that I almost hit but managed to avoid. I barely missed a tree as I skidded off the road, had a time explaining the resulting transmission trouble to my machinist." I blinked quickly, and looked up at the room's tapestried walls. "Poor furry bugger, I couldn't hurt him just because I'd had a rough day."

Mr. Braeburn nodded. "Of course. That squirrel was not meeting your wife every Tuesday."

I stood up from my chair. "Look here, Braeburn, I don't like what you're getting at."

"Please, Mr. Rafferty, sit. Sit."

I grudgingly obliged. "I must say I don't understand what squirrels and video games have to do with choosing my method of suicide."

"Choosing your proposed method of premature life evacuation," Braeburn corrected.

"Whatever the devil, I thought I was here to help form a plan."

"That you are, old chap, that you are." Braeburn rifled through a few pages on the table before him. "We have taken the liberty of researching Mr. Percy Ambrose's daily habits."

I could not help but raise an eyebrow. "Have you now?"

Mr. Braeburn nodded. "He leaves his rooms weekdays at 7am on the dot. He walks north on Spring and buys a paper from the sidewalk stand at Spring and Sentry. He scans the headlines, folds the paper under his arm and continues on to Midfield Avenue, where he waits two and one-thirds minutes for the crossing light."

"Infernal intersection," I mumbled.

Braeburn nodded. "I agree, an underground crosswalk should be tunneled there. In any event, he then strays from the most efficient route to his office; a left on Corson would shave five, six minutes from his commute."

"Where does he go?" I asked, with not a little impatience.

"Straight on Midfield, past a small gardened park. The sidewalk curves around the park and yields onto a small, quiet sidestreet where Mr. Ambrose nonetheless stops and looks both ways before crossing."

I could feel my brow furrowing. "Where does that leave him?"

"At the Rise 'N Shine Cafe & Bakery, where every day he orders a hazelnut latte and tips Pamela, the morning barrista, one Euro."

I found myself again rising from my seat. "A Euro? Every day? Does Corbella know about this Pamela woman?"

Braeburn hesitated. "I do not know, we have not researched her or her relationship to your wife."

"Well you bloody well should, since this clown apparently cannot keep his libido in check!"

Braeburn reached over and patted my knee. "I fear we are losing focus, Mr. Rafferty. The point of our research is that Mr. Ambrose obtains his coffee, then opens his paper and reads it while walking across Argon Street."

I cocked my head. "He reads while crossing an intersection?"

Braeburn nodded. "It's a very small street, virtually a bicycle path."

"But cars may drive down it?"

"They do, occasionally. Not often, at that hour of the morning."

I formed an image of my mind as a series of gears, and watched a clump of rust fall as two large pieces of metal rotated against each other.

"Tell me your plan," I said to Mr. Braeburn.

A detailed map of my London neighborhood was plopped before me.

"Your roadster can achieve top speed in less than a kilometer," Braeburn said. "From your townhome garage, you can take Ellwyn to Midfield, then twist around on Cornwell to hit Argon."

I nodded, the movements of Braeburn's finger blurring on the map. "Where am I going, then?"

"Why, to kill Mr. Ambrose, of course."

I remember the sharp scent of acrid fumes before my eyes focused on Mr. Braeburn's piercing blue gaze.

"Mr. Rafferty? Are you sentient?" he asked.

I coughed. "I believe so, good man. What happened?"

"You fainted, sir, completely out of the blue," said Braeburn, capping a vial of smelling salts.

"Sorry about that, don't know what came over me. What did I miss?"

"We were discussing Mr. Ambrose. Your running into him at high speed."

I slumped back in my chair and motioned for Braeburn to continue speaking.

"It looks to be a very clean hit; he'll either roll up onto your hood or simply fall to the pavement where your wheels will finish him off."

I allowed Braeburn's words to sink in. "But…then what? Do I stop and make sure he's dead?"

Braeburn considered this a moment. "I suppose you could back up over him once or twice before moving on, that should do the trick."

I reached forward for my cup of cooling tea. "I do not wish to appear difficult, Mr. Braeburn, but while the thought of Mr. Ambrose's demise is, by any means, somewhat pleasurable, I must say this plan seems to lack—well, the means for my demise."

Mr. Braeburn released a short bark of laughter. "You do keep your eyes on the prize, don't you? I'm getting to that part of the plan, sir, but it depends upon your receptivity to the mowing down of Mr. Ambrose with your car."

I pursed my lips and nodded. "I can live with that."

Braeburn laughed again. "But can you die with that?"

I sighed. "Please, I am starting to become very confused as to where all this is going."

Braeburn leaned forward and opened up the map to feature areas outside of my own small neighborhood. "Your contract was for your own death, which we will provide within the boundaries of your life-insurance policy. We have also included the death of your nemesis, Percy Ambrose, at no extra charge."

I cleared my throat to interrupt him. "Yes, well, we haven't exactly discussed payment yet, have we, the paperwork has been vague on that point."

Braeburn lifted his opened palms with a shrug. "One half million Euro, for either just you, or you and Ambrose."

"Good God," I coughed.

"Or…" Braeburn shrugged again. "Nothing."

My eyebrows nearly touched my cheekbones as I frowned. "That's quite a leap. I suspect that 'nothing' actually comes at a price?"

Braeburn nodded. "At Braeburn-Drury, we of course realize that money means little to the practically-dead. However, we imagine it can mean a great deal to those left behind."

I pushed my teacup away with a scowl. "Name your terms, Braeburn."

"You can well afford a half million Euro, it sits liquid in your accounts as we speak. The remainder will allow your family to live in their accustomed style for one, perhaps two years, after which their standard of living will drastically change. It is money well-spent, though; you will have a noble death, and Percy Ambrose will not become stepfather to your children."

"Go on," I said through clenched teeth.

"Of course, along with Ambrose's life goes his earning power. You could, I suppose, allow him to live, and die knowing that your family will be well taken care of."

"Not an option, sir," I said.

"Well, then—your and Ambrose's demise will be free of charge if you care to perform a small task for Braeburn-Drury before your death."

My eyes, already slitted, narrowed further. "What task?"

Braeburn placed his hands on his knees before rising. "Come now, we shall need more tea before continuing—would you care to peruse this dossier while I brew another pot?"

Braeburn handed me a black file bound with a red elastic. I opened it to find another roadmap and the photographs of several middle-aged men. "What's all this?"

"Read on, read on," Braeburn said with a wave of his hand as he navigated a pot of water over a lit Bunsen Burner.

The dossier included a map of intersections marked with large X's.

"What the devil?" I said.

Braeburn returned to his seat with a glance over his shoulder at the bubbling water. "It's a lot of information, I know. Suffice to say we would like you to continue your drive after hitting Ambrose, and run over a few others. It's a prime time of the morning; everyone walking to work, busy with coffee and thoughts of the day ahead. Nate Robinson crosses Oxford Street two minutes after Ambrose's death, and provides the opportunity for another clean hit. Orville Buttbrinke walks into Thatcher Avenue a minute after that, and Neville Artting crosses Third Street moments later."

I gave an incredulous look first to the papers in my hands, then to Braeburn. "You want me to run over all of these men before I die?"

"They're on your way, shouldn't be a bother. After killing Ambrose, what's another four?"

"You named three others."

"Well, we were hoping you could also nick off Herbert Trumboldt on the curb of Teister Lane." Braeburn noticed my opened mouth. "You won't hang for any of it, old chap, we have other plans for you."

"You are insane," I said, throwing the papers down on the small table between us.

Braeburn demurred with a small tilt of his head. "Practical, Rafferty, or perhaps opportunistic. Robinson's a puppet of the new Russian Mafia, Buttbrinke and Artting work under him while maintaining their own separate black-market artillery trades. Trumboldt is perhaps the worst of the four, dealing in Eastern-European prostitutes and chemical weapons. Others will undoubtedly soon take their place, but a decisive strike like this will cause enough confusion in their ranks for our people to delay their operations for weeks, if not months."

"Your people?" I said.

Braeburn sighed. "Yes, they save the world every day, without thanks."

I cleared my throat. "And if I refuse…will your next client be charged with this task?"

Braeburn shrugged. "For this particular job, we might well have to wait a while before another suitable candidate comes along."

"And until then I assume there are many other tasks to be performed?"

Braeburn sighed. "This is a business, Rafferty. Our bread-and-butter lies mostly in the humdrum—clients who wish to die quiet, painless deaths after dismembering childhood molesters or suffocating faithless lovers, and those who wish to submit to experimental medical procedures in order for their deaths to further science. It is rare for a client to not provide a template for his or her death, rarer still for one such as you to present himself."

I snorted. "What could possibly be 'rare' about me?"

Braeburn settled back in his chair, although the water over the Bunsen Burner was roiling wildly. "You hold an inherent grudge against the world, and you like running things over."

I bristled. "Well, who doesn't?"

"You'd be surprised," said Braeburn.

I shook my head. "This is ridiculous. Why, you heard yourself how I couldn't even run over a squirrel."

Braeburn nodded. "Yes, that's a bit worrisome, but I believe killing Ambrose will deflate that hurdle."

"Ambrose is bigger than a squirrel," I pointed out.

"Yes, but he's shagging your wife."

I fell silent, my thoughts struggling against each other like capsized boaters. "I still don't see what makes me different from your other clients."

Braeburn sighed. "You actually applied to MI5 and Scotland Yard."

I looked down at the Persian rug beneath us. "I was a bit of a maverick in my youth, had delusions of saving the world."

"From Communists?" Braeburn smiled. "That job's been taken care of. Terrorism seems a trend likely to last, but there are already quite enough agencies devoted to that particular evil. No, your interests lie in the more subtle world of corporate international espionage."

"They do?" I asked.

"I believe so. The abuses of pharmaceutical companies, the buying out of ever-larger companies by a handful of financial behemoths?"

"It's disgraceful," I said, with heat.

"It is, indeed. Here at Braeburn-Drury we do not operate under the auspices of 'good' or 'evil'—those are relative terms with no value in regards to business. If any activity was to be described as dastardly, it would be the monopolization of the world's environmental, intellectual and industrial resources."

"Are you fighting against this, then? By killing these men?" I asked.

Braeburn paused. "Yes."

I sat still for a time, during which Braeburn prepared a sweet, milky cup of tea and placed it in my hands.

"My own death…" I began.

Braeburn indicated the dossier. "The last page. You can read it later."

The light outside the apartment's bay window stepped off dusk's curb into twilight.

"I will perform your task," I said.

Braeburn nodded. "I will assemble the paperwork."

The following week offered a series of surreptitiously delivered instructions from Braeburn: Please ensure the roadster has a full tank of petrol. When convenient, please check that all turning signals are in working order. Your Monday morning breakfast should be light, with substantial protein. There was also a directive to perform fifty daily push-ups, which perplexed me; perhaps Braeburn believed this activity would hone my reflexes. I permitted myself to note, with a twinge of chagrin, that my only successful incentive for exercise to date was in preparation for a homicidal rampage culminating in my own demise.

I perhaps ill-used my last days by cloistering myself in the den watching dvds of Prime Suspect, leaving the house only for ridiculously rich meals at expensive restaurants I had previously neglected to patronize. Corbella did not notice a change in my behavior during this week; if anything, she seemed relieved that I bothered her less than usual. My sons also used this time to attend to school projects and friends without paternal interference. My home exuded an aura of peace and freedom I had not felt in it for years, and this cemented my resolution to end my life.

Alone on Sunday evening, I pried the black dossier from between my mattress and boxspring. Corbella was 'out,' with Ambrose, I assumed; the children were sleeping over with school friends. My mind wandered a moment back to university, trying to place an author with the grim pronouncement that we all die alone. I snapped off the red elastic, flipped through the businessmen's biographies and scanned the 'X'd London map I had virtually memorized; the only page of the dossier I had left to read was the last one.

I should have read it earlier, I mused; I might have done something different with my last week, or at least increased my push-ups. I thought, for a moment, how I held in my hands the answer to the greatest question most people have about their lives. The exact time and method of my death lay under a colorful map of London, where an illustrated choo-choo waved up at me from King's Cross Station.

My index finger shook once before I willed it to stop. I remembered my mother, now dead, beaming as I led her through the dusty renovations of my then newly-purchased townhome. Corbella had kissed me in the foyer as a section of ceiling plaster fell at our feet, the empty hall ringing with our laughter. I blinked, and returned from ten years past to the finished tomb of my bedroom. I flipped the London map over to reveal the dossier's last page.

It was blank.

On Monday, I gunned the roadster in my garage at 6:52AM. The garage door raised, and I pulled out onto the street. This morning was to go as planned, for my ill and my family's good.

I drove down Ellwyn and turned onto Midfield, then expertly performed the sharp turn onto Cornwell. Flower stands blazed by my roadster's windows in tufts of red and pink that blurred into butcher shops and shoe stores. I waited a few seconds at a street light, then made a left on Argon.

Argon was a tight street of ancient cobblestones where artists and heroin dealers had recently been displaced to make room for renovated townhomes and franchised bookshops. These flashed by as I accelerated toward the intersection presided over by the Rise 'N Shine Bakery.

Ambrose was there, stepping off the curb with his nose in the morning paper and a hazelnut latte held in his left hand; he was young and handsome, even while schlepping to work. For a moment, I imagined his floppy hair and smiling face in wedding photographs with Corbella, in Cancun or somesuch, my young sons throwing sand at each other on a sunset beach. I blinked these images away, revved the roadster's motor, and ran over Percy Ambrose.

He didn't have a second to acknowledge me, the roadster was that quick; he perhaps read Barnes & Noble stock up two points today, then saw a flash of stars before darkness. He disappeared under my hood and I screeched to a halt, then backed up to hear the satisfying sound of flesh under wheels. I accelerated forward and in my rearview mirror saw a rumpled mass of humanity in the road behind me; Ambrose was dead, for sure. I focused my eyes ahead, and sped toward Oxford Street.

I recognized Nate Robinson from his dossier photograph; doughy lips, a peaked nose and black trenchcoat. He stood in the crosswalk of Oxford Street, waving to someone on the sidewalk. The cars in the lane next to me sat motionless before the intersection's red light, but I motored through it and watched Robinson's body bounce up over my hood and onto the roof of my car before falling into the street behind me.

Car horns blared and pedestrians shouted as I turned onto Thatcher Avenue. Orville Buttbrinke's eyes widened in the intersection as he waved his arms, but I didn't stop the roadster. I plowed into him, and heard a spongy smack against my grill. My progress was slowed by the roadster's left front wheel grinding against sinew; I backed up for momentum to break free and continued on.

Tiester Lane appeared before me, and I saw a man answering Herbert Trumboldt's description hanging off the curb. With cat-like reflexes, he jumped back onto the sidewalk as I swerved to hit him.

"Bollocks!" I cursed to myself. I heard Braeburn's strained voice in my memory: If complications arise, revert to Plan B. I parked the roadster and pulled a pearl-handled gun from the glove box.

"Blind fucker!" Trumboldt screamed as I exited the roadster.

"Be quiet, man," I said, showing him my pistol.

"I will not, you fucking git!" Trumboldt shouted at me.

"It's a bit early for that kind of language, don't you think?" I asked.

"Not too early for you to almost kill me, you ignorant fuck!"

"Now, now, Mr. Trumboldt," I said.

He became still as a statue at the mention of his name. "I don't know you."

"Nor do I know you," I said, and raised my pistol.

"Stop!" Trumboldt held his splayed hands before me like the jazz hands of my niece in her school dance recital last year.

"What is it now?" I sighed. I felt my tweed car-coat from J. Crew whip most fashionably about my knees in the strong morning breeze.

"Who hired you?" Trumboldt asked.

"I work alone," I replied. I hadn't anticipated this degree of theatricality in my contract with Braeburn-Drury, and thought ruefully that my best investment had been my last.

Trumboldt smiled. "You're Braeburn's lackey."

My pearl-handled pistol wavered a moment.

Trumboldt placed his thumbs in his belt loops and chuckled. "It's true, he didn't have the guts to kill me himself."

"You, sir…must die," I said, waving the pistol at him.

"And why's that?" laughed Trumboldt.

My mind scanned the memorized black dossier. "Eastern-European prostitution ring and sale of chemical weapons."

Trumboldt nearly choked on his mirth. "I visit prostitutes, but I'm just a tax man."

I puffed up my chest. "Who sells chemical weapons to questionable clients."

Trumboldt's knees were now bent. "Stop, I'm going to piss myself!"

I fired the gun. Its bullet shot a pinstriped section of cloth off Trumboldt's left thigh.

He looked at me with wonder, then pain. "You clueless motherfucker."

I fired again, and his left shoulder snapped back.

"Oww," Trumboldt said.

I could hear several sirens approaching, what sounded like both ambulance and police cars. I pulled Trumboldt from the pavement and pushed him into the roadster.

"Talk," I said, using my right hand to drive and the left to hold my pistol to Trumboldt's temple.

"Braeburn's going to kill you," Trumboldt said.

"Of course he's going to kill me, that's what I paid him for!"

Trumboldt blinked up at me. "You're a suicide?"

I pursed my lips, and continued driving.

"He's not what he says, is all," Trumboldt said. "Half of his business is legit, the other he uses to further his own means."

"He's saving the world!" I shouted, as I ran a red light.

"Fuck, man, you're an idiot!"

I pressed the pearl-handled pistol closer to Trumboldt's head. "Why's that?"

"Braeburn is saving Braeburn, not the sodding world."

We were passing warehouses next to the Thames, and I pulled into a greasy alley where I embraced Trumboldt's neck in a chokehold. "I'm dying today no matter what, and I'm to take you with me. You're making me late for my destiny. If you have something to say, say it."

"Braeburn's not going to kill you," Trumboldt said.

My arm twitched, but still held onto Trumboldt's neck. "More."

"He's going to make you a patsy for several crimes and leave you for MI5, that'll take attention away from his own affairs for a while."

"How do you know this?" I asked.

Trumboldt sighed. "I went to Braeburn-Drury for a suicide myself."

I slumped back in my seat, and let my pistol fall.

Trumboldt winced, and felt his shoulder. "The 'task' added to your own demise, the black dossier with the last page blank?"

I started, and brought the pistol to his forehead. "No. I will free the world from corporate dominance, then die painlessly."

Trumboldt laughed. "You'll rot in prison, and have your ass reamed daily."

Sirens sounded again, distant yet insistent.

"Where were you supposed to go?" Trumboldt asked. "A warehouse a few blocks from here?"

I nodded, against my will.

Trumboldt coughed, pink spittle landing on the roadster's steering wheel. "Braeburn won't be there, but MI5 will."

I turned to my captive. "I really think that you do sell chemical weapons."

Trumboldt grinned. "How else can I afford all of those prostitutes?"

I smiled back, then shot him in the face.

I had never ridden on the large Ferris Wheel next to the Thames, but watched it now as I waited for Braeburn to approach; his bowler hat appeared out of nowhere.

"It's time, isn't it, man?" he said.

"Seems like." I found myself, like presumably countless others before me, wishing for a last cigarette even though I hadn't smoked for twenty years. The ever-increasing background noise of sirens distracted my thoughts.

"You went above and beyond, with that Trumboldt nonsense."

"Yes, hadn't expected that," I said.

"Up on the edge, man," Braeburn said, indicating the nearest piling. I obediently obliged.

Braeburn nodded. "You did a good service for all; your family, your country, yourself."

"I did good, as the Americans say," I shrugged.

"Any last words for Corbella?"

"Yes." I looked down at the churning waters of the Thames, then met Braeburn's eyes. "Good-bye," I said, then pulled the trigger of my pearl-handled pistol one last time.

Braeburn's blue eyes filled with blood. I glanced over my shoulder at the line of black MI5 vans approaching, then stepped out into nothingness, a cold fog cloaking me as I fell into liquid grey absolution.

✗

EVERETT TRUE   **BY CONDO**

THE HOT STOVE LEAGUE

by Janice Law

I'm already seated, and Mal, my producer, is yakking in my ear about the points he wants me to cover, while Luis fiddles with his cameras and fusses as always about too much light on my face. I can't help it if I am going bald; he'll just have to deal with it. Drink of water, my mouth is dry. I have been waiting for this moment for a long time, preparing, you might say, since I was nineteen. Was nineteen right? Yes, it was winter, the winter I turned nineteen and played on the first line with Roman Martineau and Tom Delacort.

How long ago that seems. I count off one to ten and run through the start of my introduction: Good evening hockey fans. This is Andy Becker with tonight's Hot Stove League. I could do that intro in my sleep and probably do, complete with the rising intonation starting with "tonight."

Mal gives me the thumbs up. This is an important program, the kickoff for the new season, and Delacort, my old junior teammate, is an important interview. He's just been elected to the Hall of Fame, and everyone is remembering his long and distinguished career: Two Stanley Cups, three times leading scorer, a perennial top ten points leader, a prince of the ice, for sure.

I've been remembering him, too, not that I had ever forgotten him. No way that was possible. I watched his career professionally, I've called his games, I can even say, honestly, that Tommie has haunted my dreams. And in a few minutes he will come through the studio door and sit down opposite me for a chat.

About some great old games—that's our format. We show clips from the classics, followed by a condensed version of a home team game from the previous season. Not that many people will want more of this last season, which was not a vintage year by any means. But with careful editing we can make a bad year look better. There are always good goals, exciting saves, big hits, plus a few fights for savor.

That's our formula and the station would have our heads if we departed from it. Don't tinker with success, I say, but tonight is special. This is a night I've been waiting for since I was nineteen, and now I'm bald enough so that Luis is calling for a little more powder and adjusting the lights.

What have we got on tap tonight? Just the usual with a twist. I've tracked down some films, that's how ancient we're talking here, with some nice footage of our junior team, when we were all eighteen or nineteen and set to conquer the world—or at least pro hockey. I think Tommie will be surprised.

Of course, we have our usual game in an hour, too, a little stinker from last November when we pulled out a win at the last moment. I remember it was a rotten game, full of hooking and holding and giveaways and every mistake in the book—even some that they invented on the spot.

We could shrink this one to fifteen minutes, and it would still be too long by ten, so I don't think there will be complaints if the interview runs longer than usual, not if it's as interesting as this one is sure to be. Even after all my years in the booth and on the set, I am excited about this one.

Mal's in my ear again and now he holds up his five fingers to give the lead-in signal. Five, four, three, two, one: "Good evening, hockey fans. This is Andy Becker with tonight's Hot Stove League. Our November 5, 2009, game against the Flyers is coming up later, but first we have tonight's guest, Tom Delacort."

I stand up and turn toward the entrance to the studio. There's my old junior linemate, a dubious human being but an icon of the sport and six feet of mighty fine hockey player. I clasp his hand and he gives me a hug. That was Tommie; there was a disconnect between what he was and how he acted. I'm told he is beloved in his hometown, which just goes to show you.

"Tommie!" I say, and he sits down and crosses one leg over the other as cool as can be. How many interviews has he done over the years? Thousands, absolutely, and he is master of all media arts. I know a pro when I see one.

We start out easy, talking about the Hall of Fame. This was the first year he was eligible, and, of course, he was a shoe-in, but Tommie's modest—or pretends to be. "I left everything up to the voters," he says. I wonder if politics are in his future.

"Well," I say on cue from Mal, "we can show the fans the evidence. Remember this?" It's a clip from his first season in the NHL. The picture is a little grainy, but there is no mistaking the Northern Express tearing down the left hand side. He was slower off the mark than his old center, Roman, but once Tommie got going there was no stopping him.

No stopping that slap shot, either. "Whew!" I say. "You don't see too many shots like that." And we're off, reminiscing. That's the essence of our Hot Stove show. The geezers love it, and the kids look at the old champs and pick up a tip or two or think how much smaller they were without the aid of modern pharmaceuticals and weight training. Those we don't discuss.

No, straight to the Stanley Cup triumphs. There's Tommie lifting the cup. Big smile—you can see the gap where he's missing a few teeth. That's Cup One. By Cup Two, he's playing with a mouth guard and has expensive dentistry. I notice stuff like that; I have an eye for detail that has kept me employed among the statisticians and analysts.

Time to go back a little. "You've seen Tom Delacort in the NHL, but let's see where he came from. Remember this, Tommie?" It's a clip from early in our last season, and I had to get the technical people to work over the film to produce a decent few minutes. There's our line, me on the right, Tommie on the left, and, in the center, Roman, one of the gods of sport.

Oh, yes. If Tommie was the prince, you had to go up the ladder a few more rungs to get to Roman. Big, but agile, fastest man on the team, and what a sweet shot! While Roman was on the team, the scouts had eyes for no one else. For sure, they knew Tommie was good and that I was fine at that level, but Roman was something else.

A good something else, too. Sports are tough. You grow up getting cheered—or booed—and nothing you do off the ice seems as important as what shows up on the scoreboard. It's easy to think you're the most important guy in the world or to get seriously down or involve yourself with easy, exciting activities you'd been better to leave alone. I know.

Roman was great without vanity, a generous soul who inspired love as well as admiration. We all wanted to be him as a player, big and brave and skillful. And in our secret hearts, we wanted his goodness, which seemed, on days when we were feeling mean and envious, an added, unfair gift, as if the gods not only play favorites but enjoy rubbing our noses in it. I think Tommie, the only one who really approached his talent, felt that the most.

I keep my eye on him as the screen fills with our youthful selves. It was a big game against our traditional provincial rivals. There's Tommie breaking up an attacking rush. The puck's momentarily loose, then Roman's on it, one stride, two, a pass to yours truly, who knew well enough to give it right back so that Roman could rifle it into the upper right corner of the net. Sticks in the air as our teammates on the bench pound the boards.

"A great play, a great game," I say. I don't add, as I could well have, that that's what genius on ice looks like.

"For sure," Tommie says, but he doesn't look comfortable. "Roman"—and he hesitates as if he'd actually forgotten the name. No way.

"Martineau," I say, perhaps a mistake, for he recovers himself in that instant. Tommie always had quick reactions.

"Modern fans won't know Roman," he says, "but he was a great player."

"He'd have perhaps been the number one draft pick off this sort of play." Roman's on the screen again, muscling the puck out of the corner; he's half knocked off his skates, but still well balanced enough to make a pass to Tommie who's in front of the net. "He made everyone look better," I said.

"The best junior center I ever saw," said Tommie. Emphasis on junior.

Well, who can blame him for that? "Roman Martineau's still remembered at home," I say. "Did you know they've named the new rink for him? The opening was a really nice ceremony."

"I didn't. I wish I'd known. I'd like to have gone."

This is a patent lie, but I let it slide. The naming of the rink is safe ground for him. "It was much deserved," I said, although Mal is hollering in my ear that the interview is Tom Delacort, not some kid no one's ever heard of fifty miles outside of Ottawa. I ignore him and recall Roman's junior career stats. "What a first line we had that championship year. Sixty goals for Roman, forty for you; I kicked in ten or eleven myself."

"You're not kidding. He'd have played NHL for sure."

"And when you think that Roman never finished the season. What was he—three weeks short?"

"Three weeks, I think. I think it was late February—or even early March?"

"The mildest spell on record. I remember that," I said. We'd never have been out at the lake otherwise, and the little tavern where we tanked up on beers and shots would not have been open, either. But it was a mild day with ice fishermen out, and we went to the lake to drink and to fool around on the ice with our sticks.

Kids were used to playing outdoors then. With the team set to clinch the division and challenge for the Cup, our coaches would have thrown a fit, worried about twigs and branches half buried in the ice and stones on the surface, all good chances to turn an ankle or take a bad fall. We thought of nothing but the chance to sneak a few beers and spend the afternoon goofing off in our favorite way on a super big sheet of ice.

I mention outdoor skating, the ancestral memory behind the new craze for the outdoor Winter Classic, and though I can see Tommie is uneasy, he's brave, I'll always give him that. "Oh, sure," he says, "best skating in the world."

"The lake was the best," I say. I can see it now, a great, blue white sheet extending to the horizon. Get up a head of steam on that and you felt that you could glide forever, free of everything. We set up two four on four teams with a pile of coats at each end for the goals, and pretty soon we were red faced, but not cold at all. A beautiful day.

"Good ice," says Tommie.

"Mostly," I say now, because it was the mildest late winter anyone remembered, and there were patches where the black water was visible beneath thin crusts of ice like cracked sheets of glass. "The thaw came early that year. I think it was after Dougie put his skate through that we went to the Fish Shack." That was the tavern, a crumbling log cabin with a pot-bellied stove and welcome kegs of Labatts.

"We had a few drinks there!" he laughs. Tommie thinks fast; he didn't get those Stanley Cup rings for nothing. He's off about sneaking booze on the team bus and after hours beer parties when we were on the road. Hot Stove stuff. "For you juniors out there, not the best idea!" he says.

Not for us, either. I'm not sure how it started, not after all these years, and back in the moment, our heads were too full of suds and self-importance. Anyway, there we are still in our skates, standing around the stove with beers in our hands when in come—now just who were they? Emissaries of Fate, sure, but in their earthly form, ice fishermen? Hikers? More skaters? Must have been. They had skates with them in any case. Or maybe the tavern rented skates. I ask Tommie, but he doesn't remember. "Maybe," he says. "And there was a place nearer the main road."

That's right. Put our memories together and we'll work it out. We will. Mal's in my ear and the lights of the studio are in my eyes, but I'm back at the tavern, watching the red eye of the stove and listening to Tommie brag about our prospects in the Cup. He's got us winning our division already, which sets off the newcomers, who are older, bigger and stronger, too, I'd guess.

One thing leads to another and there's some pushing and shoving before Claude, that's the bartender, told us to go settle it outside. Some evil genius suggested a game, though the light was fading and the floodlight in front of the tavern didn't extend very far, and we've all had more beer than was good for us.

Tommie's remembering, too. He looks pale but determined. "It was a game, a friendly pickup game. But they'd been drinking."

"Us, too." And I think, in vino veritas.

Same set up, coats for goals, but close to the shore for the benefit of the light. To the west, the sky turned gold and sank into purple streaks, and the ice reflected blue and rose. It was a rough game. No boards, of course, but lots of open ice hits. Our opponents were bigger, but not nearly as skilled, and Tommie was showing off by eluding their checks and using his quick stick work to trip up their forwards.

Pretty soon there was a nasty edge to the game, and if we'd been smart, we'd have packed it in and all had another round in the tavern like good buddies. Roman, who had the clout, should have called play dead, and normally he would have. But his weakness was that he had no head for alcohol. Not a lot of taste for it, either, though he'd have a couple of beers to go along with the rest of us and pretty soon he'd be singing *Frere Jacques* off key, or, in really daring moods, attempting *American Pie*.

So Roman was pretty well out of it, but still gliding effortlessly around the ice. I think left to himself, he'd still have brought them 'round. Anyone seeing him had to love his skating, had to love the way he moved.

Instead, there was a dust up on the ice. "You butt-ended their center," I say to Tommie.

"He hit me from behind," Tommie replies, not so careful now; I can see that he's back with me at the lake in the red and purple twilight with the sound of blades on ice.

Two of them took off after him, but Tommie raced down the improvised rink, past the pile of coats and out onto the darkening lake, fast, fast. Roman saw what was happening. He pivoted and followed, his big strides closing the gap, the rest of us following behind or engaging in ice fistfights with our opponents.

"They cut me off," Tommie says. Yes, we saw that. At least one of them was a fast skater and possibly sober. That was cheating, wasn't it?

Straggling after them, we saw Tommie cut toward the shore, saw a group of skaters, surely more than two, three or four at least, after him, plus Roman, closing fast now. They swept near the rocks, and it looked as if Tommie lost his edge, for he tumbled to the ice. He was on his knees instantly, swinging his stick and sending one of his pursuers to the ice and another sliding against the rocks to keep his balance.

He took a nasty hit from behind, though, before Roman joined the fray. We were skating fast as we could, but they were in the shadow of the rocks and trees, and later no one could say for sure what he'd seen. Just bodies, just dark silhouettes against the night and the ice. I remember yelling—we're coming! Or maybe a warning, and then I was grappling with some stranger—how stupid it all was, people we'd not even met before.

Roman was clearing a swath on the ice, and then he fell. "He was hit with a stick," Tommie says. "And fell badly. He must have hit a rock. There was water, too. He was found with his face in water."

There's a sharp, hysterical edge to his voice; I can hear it underneath the control that comes with long experience. Mal can hear it, too, for he stops trying to direct and shuts up.

"Roman might have survived," I say, "if we had acted quick enough."

"It was chaos," Tommie says, more confident now. "I didn't realize he was hurt at first. Everyone yelling. And those guys—what the hell were they thinking? They scattered all over the ice."

"We heard their truck start up," I say. I remember lights sweeping over the ice, for night had come down while we threw punches and wrestled around and let our friend die.

"He was lying behind—was it a rock or a big tree limb? Sticking half out of the ice, wasn't it?" Tommie in reminiscent mode. Well, we were all at fault there. Standing around congratulating each other, until someone said, Roman made short work of them, and then we realized he wasn't standing in the shadows with us and we started to call him, joking at first: You can come out now!

"I thought he'd gone after them," Tommie says. "He was never afraid of a fight."

"It must have been a good five minutes," I say.

"At least. It was lack of oxygen in the end, wasn't it?"

We all know that. We read the coroner's report. Hell, we were at the inquest. "But there were questions," I say.

"Always." Tommie's face is smooth; he thinks we're over the dangerous bit, that we've slid past the thin ice of memory.

"No one could identify the other guys in the truck."

"Never. I'd never seen them. Not the barkeep, either."

"Smart of them," I say, "given the injury. Roman had been struck in the temple. That's why he collapsed and went through that weak place in the ice." There had been a little stream there, and the running water kept the ice thin.

"The police did everything they could," says Tommie, as if I'm criticizing the province's finest. I think again that politics might be in his future, and suddenly I have no regrets at all.

"He'd been kicked, while he was down on the ice. Just once in the melee."

Tommie looks pale again despite the studio makeup. "As you say, in the melee. People flailing around, falling, kicking out."

"You," I say. "It was you, not the strangers, no one else."

Mal goes ballistic in my ear, and Tommie isn't much calmer. A lawyer's mentioned and I think my old linemate is going to come across the table at me, but I shake my head. "I was the slowest man on our line," I say. "No hockey superstar, but I stayed on the line because I noticed everything. Off ice, too. Getting into the cars, right? We sat with the doors open or leaned against the side to take off our skates. And I saw your left skate had blood on the tip."

"There was blood on the ice," Tommie yells. "Blood on our hands."

"There was blood on the tip of your skate, not on the blade, not on the shoe, not on the laces. One quick kick and you were the star of the show and the big draft choice and the one all the scouts were dying to see."

"You're crazy! We're talking thirty years ago almost. If you'd thought that, you'd have spoken up, raised the roof, told the police."

"Thirty years ago I was nineteen and scared. Ten minutes later the skate was wiped clean—yes, I checked—and there was no way to prove anything, not with the biggest game of our lives coming up. Not when everyone expected us to win the Cup for Roman."

"And now what are you getting out of it, Andy, but a libel suit and a whole lot of flack?" He was himself again free of memory and bad ice, Tom Delacort, hockey icon and Hall of Fame resident.

"Now I'm going to get proof," I say. "The story about your Hall of Fame election got me thinking. You donated all your skates— every pair from junior to your final game for a special exhibition, Evolution of the Modern Skate, right? They can tell now, Tommie. Even after all these years, they can tell if it was Roman's blood on the point of your left skate, and if it was—" I say, but I don't get to finish.

My old linemate has knocked the coffee table aside and gone for me. I'm on the floor and getting pounded, but I don't care— I've owed Roman this for a long time, and I've accrued plenty of interest. Mal comes out of the booth and the second cameraman starts wrestling with Tommie, but Luis, bless him, is still behind his lens, and we're getting all of this recorded. I feel blood in my mouth, and I'll lose a tooth for sure, but this is one for Roman, and a Hot Stove League Show no one will forget.

✗

THE COIN AND THE CHEMIST

by Nijo Philip

It was 2:50 p.m. on a Friday when I stopped to stare at the constellation Orion painted on the ceiling of Grand Central Terminal. The luminous windows towered stoically as crowds of commuters swirled across the Main Concourse like dry leaves in a chaotic October wind.

"I think I lost him," said Enzo, adjusting his blazer and scanning the pedestrians at the train station.

"You sure his face was pink?" I asked. "Like a ham?" I didn't doubt Enzo's skills of observation, but a man with a pink face would stand out even in a large crowd.

"I expect trouble," said Enzo. "You still want to come along?"

I nodded. "We're partners, Enzo. Don't forget it."

"Let's move it, Jack," he said. "If I'm right, a man named James Marshall is in a lot of danger."

The 3:01 p.m. Metro-North growled impatiently at the platform. Enzo and I found seats facing each other while a group of German tourists boarded and sat on the far end of the car drinking beers. Around us, people read newspapers and worked on laptops. The Metro-North beat against the tracks with a crescendo, hurrying us to our destination.

Minutes went by as we listened to the clamor of the passengers and ticket collectors. After our tickets were punched, Enzo told me the details.

"A woman named Emily Marshall asked me to check on her father, James Marshall, a retired chemist in the town of Chappaqua, in Westchester. She hadn't heard from him in days, which is unlike him—at the very least, they call each other once a day—so she drove up to check on the house. Mr. Marshall never answered the door; instead, he opened the second floor window.

"Hey, you listening Jack?"

I was distracted by the Germans who started doing impersonations of De Niro, Brando, and Eastwood.

"I'm listening Enzo. Keep talking."

"Well, this Marshall, usually a cheery man, pounded his fists on the window sill at seeing his daughter. She had never seen him look so angry. He said he was busy and she was disturbing him. She asked if she could go inside but he was so inflamed that he told her to go away, and shut the window."

"So her father sent her away. Big deal."

Enzo looked perturbed. "She did alert the local police, and Marshall had opened the door for them and they reported no problems other than Marshall's cranky demeanor. Emily is a part-time nurse and she returned to Manhattan to make a home visit with a client."

I opened a notebook and tried to keep up with the facts of the case.

"Doesn't sound like anything is wrong," I said. "What are you going to do, Enzo, win her father's love back for her?"

Enzo leaned forward. "Jack, you're not seeing the point. All of this coincides with something else. Emily said for the past few days, she's seen a man with a pink face following her."

Enzo leaned back into the cushion of the chair. He shut his eyes and I watched his Italian features relax.

As Harlem flickered in the window, I pulled out the company papers, and reviewed our inventory. We needed more vermicelli and canned eggplant this month.

Enzo and I had been best friends since high school. He became a cop after college while I fell in with the wrong crowd and got into some gambling problems. By the time we were in our late thirties, Enzo had a wife and he felt the pressure to leave the NYPD. As for me, I got into deeper trouble as I tried to pay for my father's hospital bills. In the end, my old man cursed me—told me I was a no good son. I was left with a huge debt and a broken heart. I had no time to mourn, however. The mafia pressured me to pay up or disappear. On the night I was to disappear, Enzo showed up with eleven police officers and saved my ass. He even paid my debt for me and got me a job at a warehouse in Brooklyn. A month later, during a routine traffic stop, Enzo was shot by a repeat offender. Enzo retired after he got out of the hospital. He made sure I stayed out of trouble, and by the time we were in our forties, we opened a food import business together. As distributors, we had plenty to keep us busy, but once in a while, Enzo's cop friends, actual detectives, would drop in to ask questions to get help on cases. The bloodhound in Enzo was very much alive. It had not been killed when he got shot. Enzo eventually advertised himself as a P.I. and took cases as a hobby—in between importing goods from Sicily and Tuscany. As the years went by, our lives became more exciting this way, and I felt that Enzo was the closest person to me, the brother I never had. I wasn't Italian, but Enzo took me into his Italian family. It was a debt I could never repay. Enzo had saved my life, and on the more dangerous cases, I followed him—to make sure he got home safely to his wife.

Enzo was alert forty minutes later as the train pulled into Chappaqua Station. The sky was ominously bright and clear; and the picturesque town below it was bustling with pedestrians and cars. A cold breeze chilled me as a young lady with freckles met us in front of a café on the main street across from the train station. Emily Marshall, I guessed. She looked like she was approaching thirty (and approaching it well). A yellow sheath dress wrapped her body tightly. She flipped a coin to Enzo, which he caught as he introduced me: "This is my friend, Jack Kamien."

I bowed my head and summoned my gentleman's voice. "Hope we didn't keep you waiting, my dear." I tried kissing her hand but she pulled it away and patted me on the head like I was a dog.

"I just got here," said Emily.

Enzo shook his head. "I would say you've been here for about twenty-three minutes. You parked your car, and then you went to the post office down the street and you just got back."

Emily's mouth dropped. "Were you following me?"

Enzo said matter-of-factly, "That white SUV belongs to you; it has your initials E.M. as part of the license plate number, and it's the only vehicle I see with a stethoscope on the dash, from your nursing job, of course. The spot you parked in is a half-hour meter and has only seven minutes remaining. So twenty-three minutes have gone by."

Emily looked at her SUV as if the truck had told Enzo all her secrets.

"You're holding a receipt for a money order, and a clean book of stamps, both newly purchased from the post office." Enzo smiled.

Emily bounced up and down, thrilled like a child by a magician. She was speechless and stared at Enzo and then looked to me as if I could explain his strange ways.

"He's always doing that," I said. "Annoying, isn't it?"

Emily ignored my comment and clapped her hands. She looked Enzo up and down. "If the police did miss anything about my dad, I'm sure you'll notice it."

"I've already noticed some things," said Enzo. He studied the markings on the coin. "From the Nguyen dynasty, I think. At that time, Chinese and Vietnamese coins were used together."

"There's a bunch more of these coins," said Emily, unlocking the doors to the SUV. "The coins are actually from different historical periods. Some have a terra-cotta casting core and come in the shape of knives or spades. Some have circles or squares cut into them. All are valuable. You think this has something to do with my father's behavior?"

"Absolutely," said Enzo. "I found an article from the American Numismatic Association about your father. James Marshall purchased one of the finest collections of rare Chinese currency from an unknown source back in 1975. Some cross referencing led me to a man named Armando Sutter, who, for a short time before your father's purchase, owned an exotic collection of Chinese currency. Your father and this man worked together for a chemical company before you were born. I'm certain your father got the coins from this man, and now he's come to reclaim it."

"But who is this man?" asked Emily.

"Sutter was a world traveler and an enthusiast of treasure hunting. I couldn't find a photo or an address of this Sutter, maybe if I had more time. But I called a contact of mine who told me that Armando Sutter is a man with a tainted record; dismissed charges of assault, fraud, theft, embezzlement; somehow, nothing ever stuck. Then in 2003, the man literally disappeared from the planet."

Emily bit her lips and thought for a while. "But none of this explains Dad becoming angry overnight," she said. "He's always open to me."

Emily drove us up winding hills, past antique shops, old bookstores, and cafés. The town of Chappaqua was painted red and yellow with fall foliage; Halloween ghosts and jack-o-lanterns loitered on the stoops of many houses.

"We're almost there," she said. We turned onto a long uphill road, and Emily slammed the vehicle to a stop. Through the glass, we saw an enormous man standing on the side of the road by an old red car. He peered into our truck, and I'll never forget those large black fish-like eyes. He quickly looked away, but not before I saw the rest of the horror that was his face; the features of his bald head were corrugated and pink, much like a burn victim.

"Keep driving," said Enzo. A moment later, through the back windshield, Enzo and I watched the man aim a gun at us, but as we made distance, he put his arms down. "That's our pink-faced man who's been watching you, Emily. He's been tailing me too, since you got in touch with me. I have to get to your father's house before this guy. Does your father have a safe?"

"He keeps valuables in a wall safe in his study, behind a Luca Giordano painting," said Emily.

"Ah, Luca Giordano. My parents liked his work," said Enzo. "I'm sure I'll recognize it."

At the Marshall property, Enzo stepped out of the truck and pulled short range binoculars from his pocket and observed the house on the hill. Black crows landed near us and strutted in front of Enzo as if he should be bird watching. He put the binoculars away and the crows cawed. I could tell by his expression that danger was approaching again.

Enzo moved to the window of the SUV, reached in, and touched Emily's shoulder. "No matter what happens," he said, "do not come to the house. Drive to the police station and tell them to come here. Make them understand—the situation is very dangerous."

Enzo ran up the driveway and the autumn wind blew fiercely. As I followed Enzo, orange leaves sailed along the ground like waves on the ocean. The Marshall estate stretched farther than the eye could see, covered by woods and surrounded by hills on the gray horizon. In the center of the land stood the immense Georgian-style house and garden, lonely and out of place.

Enzo walked around the garden and came back to the front of the house and observed the windows. He rang the doorbell and whistled a tune.

The door opened. A tall man who looked like a scarecrow peered at us from inside. The long white hair on his yellow skull fell to his shoulders.

"What do you fellas want? Are you more police?" he asked.

"Not exactly. My name is Vincenzo Morcelli. I'm a private investigator."

The old man grunted with disdain and nearly had the door shut when Enzo yelled, "We were sent by your daughter. Your life is in danger."

The door didn't close, and the thin figure reappeared.

"James Marshall," said the old man offering a bony hand to Enzo. Marshall coughed; a full body writhing cough, for a full minute. Gross, I thought. He spit out a bolus of phlegm, wiped his lips and offered his hand to me, which I pretended not to notice. I occupied myself with observing the crows.

Enzo explained the situation to Marshall. He invited us inside.

Marshall's house smelled as if a window hadn't been opened in ages, but elegance was everywhere. The furniture held gently curving lines in the Hepplewhite style. Mahogany was the predominant color for display cases and tables, and decorative moldings of Rosette and Guilloché framed the doorways and even the balusters. Paintings hung on nearly every wall. And still, in the dim halls of the house, there remained the traces of its not-so-elegant occupant: chemistry books, leftover Chinese food, cigarette butts, a collection of Time magazines spilled on the floor; and coffee cups everywhere, some half empty, and others dry. I looked for a place to sit, but the sofas looked uninviting.

"I'd like to have a look around the house," said Enzo.

Marshall felt around his waist and hips, and checked his pants pockets and then looked around the room.

"Something wrong?" asked Enzo.

"I can't find my glasses," replied Marshall. "I can barely see without them." He searched the house for some time while Enzo examined a picture of the late Rose Marshall, which hung over a table that held a music box. Enzo opened the lid and the instrument played Schubert's Piano Trio No. 2.

Marshall gave up on the glasses, and he led us through the first floor of the house, to a brightly lit lab. In contrast to the antique nature of the rest of the house, the lab was very modern. The wall shelves were stocked with glass Erlenmeyer flasks, reagent bottles, stoppers, other volumetric flasks and pipettes. The table was overrun by vortex mixers, hotplates, and distillation units. Some of the burners were lit, and multi-colored liquids bubbled in various containers.

"Big place," said Enzo.

"For big ideas to become practical," said Marshall.

"I guess this is what keeps you so busy that you ignore your daughter?" asked Enzo.

Marshall wrung his hands and coughed, another wracking cough that shook his bony frame.

Enzo's gaze fell to the carpet and he followed his senses to the next room. "There's more than one set of footprints in the carpet leading this way."

"The police were here today," said Marshall. "Emily must have told you fellas."

We entered the study; a cold room lined with bookcases and wooden crates and a desk with more bottles of chemicals. A single painting hung on the walls; an oversized print of Luca Giordano's Vertumnus and Pomona.

Enzo peeked behind the frame. "What a work of art," he said. "It's a model ninety-five."

Marshall squinted his eyes. "Did Emily—"

Enzo nodded and lifted the painting down and whistled at the safe. "Amazing. The model ninety-five requires two sets of codes to gain entry."

Marshall positioned himself between the safe and Enzo.

"You don't have to worry about us," said Enzo, "it's Armando Sutter that you better watch out for."

Marshall's body quivered at the mere mention of Sutter's name. He sat down on a crate and I did the same, as there were no chairs.

"Where is Sutter?" asked Marshall, clearly distressed.

"You tell us," said Enzo, also seating himself on a crate.

"I wouldn't know. I haven't seen him in years."

"Yes, you have," Enzo asserted. Enzo pulled out the Chinese coin Emily had given him and, shoving aside some books, placed it on the table.

The old man opened his eyes wide and moved his mouth like he was thirsty. He slapped a hand to his forehead. "Listen fellas, I didn't tell the police this. I was too afraid of what Armando would do. He came around here a few days ago and wanted me to give him the rest of my currency collection. My treasure." Marshall's growly voice worked to speak through a fit of coughing.

"Sutter showed up on Monday evening, and I let him in to explain himself. He'd been hiding in Africa all these years without a dime in his pocket. He heard about the increased value of the treasure."

"Yes, you donated part of the collection to Princeton University," said Enzo.

"Unfortunately, it got publicized and revealed the true value of my collection. Sutter sold the collection to me for half a million dollars. The treasure is rarer than what anyone originally thought decades ago. The remaining coins in my safe now hold a value of eight and a half million."

Marshall coughed, and spit into a coffee cup. "Armando Sutter said he had a reasonable proposal—he wanted just half of what remains of the collection. I rejected the whole idea, and out of politeness offered him some brandy, which I went to get from the liquor cabinet. I was in the middle of work, so unfortunately, without thinking I led him to this room, and here he waited while I fetched the brandy. Well, fellas, what the hell do you think I saw when I returned?"

Enzo listened carefully.

"I saw Sutter sitting innocently, while the painting hung a few inches off level, tilted. Keep in mind, fellas, I keep that painting a particular way. I knew Armando had discovered the safe. So I threw him out. Before he walked out the door, he threatened me. 'Watch yourself,' he said, 'and don't forget, I know you have a daughter. Think it over.' Then he left. But I've been so afraid for the past few days."

Enzo slapped his knees. "Sutter's intent is to crack your safe and steal the Chinese currency."

Marshall thought it over. "I've been thinking that I should give Sutter some of the gold if it would mean he'd leave me alone. I was especially nervous today when Emily, and later, the police, showed up. If Armando Sutter knew…that's why I sent Emily away…and then you two show up."

"Armando Sutter has a close watch on you, Mr. Marshall." Enzo gazed at the Giordano painting. "Sutter will make a move soon."

Enzo's cell phone rang and in the brief conversation, a worried look came over his face. He grabbed my arm. "That was Marianna. She said little Enzo has a bad fever. She's taking him to the hospital."

I placed my hand on Enzo's shoulder. "It'll be all right, Enzo."

"Will you go, Jack? Go to the hospital and stay with my baby. You're his godfather, after all."

I wanted to do as he asked, but I wasn't going to leave Enzo alone during this investigation. I felt danger was in the air and revulsion to leaving Enzo alone. "Listen, I love Enzo Jr. as much as you, but I'm staying. He'll be in the hospital. He'll be fine."

Marshall watched Enzo with an affectionate gaze. "There's nothing like love between a father and son," he said, rubbing his chin.

We sat in silence for some minutes.

Marshall picked up the Chinese coin from the table and specks on it glittered. "Ah!" His eyes lit up. "I need to put this away!" He walked towards the safe.

Amid the howling of the October wind outside, the three of us heard a thumping from inside the house. Enzo and I froze.

Again we heard it. Thump!

Enzo remained calm and lifted his ear.

I knew danger was imminent. Thump! "Someone's in the house," I said.

Marshall hurried to the safe. "Are you sure?" he asked.

Enzo looked out the window. I breathed deeply. Enzo told me to wait behind the door. If anyone came in, I was to stop them. Marshall was busy with the safe. He punched in the access code on the small buttons. A green light sparkled to life.

Thump! The noise got louder.

He punched in the second access code. A second light turned on.

Thump!

I heard it clearly. Someone was approaching.

Thump!

Enzo backed away from the window and rushed to me. "The glasses!" shouted Enzo. "I'm so stupid."

The sound got even louder. Thump! Thump! Thump!

Marshall pressed a button and the safe door clicked open. He kissed the coin and placed it into the safe. He eyed me and Enzo. By his feet was a leather bag full of various Chinese coins. "This is such a good safe," he said, caressing the steel door.

Enzo spoke slowly. "You're right. The safe is a very good one. I trust the safe. On the other hand, I don't trust you—Armando Sutter!"

"Armando Sutter?" I yelled.

The old man snarled. He pulled his arm out of the safe and aimed a pistol at Enzo. With an innate swiftness, Enzo pulled his own gun from his coat and pointed it towards the old man. Gunshots blazed and bullets ricocheted across the room. Dust and splinters exploded, with some of it landing in my eyes. I felt a bullet whizz by my head.

"Stay down!" whispered Enzo, pressing me to the floor. He kept me down until the man emptied his gun. I wiped tears and debris out of my eyes and I smelled gunpowder. Armando Sutter was still standing by the safe, with his gun arm down. He had been shot in the arm. He stared at Enzo with hate.

Then I saw Sutter pull the knife. A rage came over me. I thought of Enzo, and his wife and child. Before I knew it, I was on top of the man, wrestling him onto his belly. Enzo rushed over and took the man's knife and gun. I pinned the man to the floor as he moaned in agony. In the distance, sirens approached.

The police broke through the door. Emily had convinced them to do so. Enzo asked the officers for a crowbar and then enlightened a rotund man with a red mustache named Detective Borkowski as to the situation at the Marshall Estate.

"For all my suspicions," said Enzo, "I never thought that Sutter would impersonate Mr. Marshall. Keep in mind that I never got a chance to see a photo of Armando Sutter, and Emily had actually seen her father at the window this morning, and due to that fact, I believed the man I encountered was James Marshall and not Sutter, the imposter."

Enzo had some of the police officers open the crates scattered about the room. Most of the men crowded around us to hear Enzo tell the story.

"Mr. Vincenzo Morcelli," said Detective Borkowski, "What made you suspect anything at all if the imposter fooled you?"

"You see," said Enzo, "the first thing that Sutter—posing as James Marshall—did when we entered the home was search for his glasses. Armando Sutter was never searching for his glasses. He meant to pull his gun on us. Here's how it went down:

"Prior to our arrival, Sutter was already in the process of stealing the treasure from the safe. He must have been holding his gun when he opened the safe and placed it in there while he started looting the treasure. When we rang the doorbell, he was more than likely caught off guard and quickly shut the safe—with the gun still inside—and came downstairs. We told him our reason for coming here, and he planned to invite us inside and shoot us, then go back to looting. When he went to draw the gun on us, he realized it wasn't tucked in the waistline of his slacks, and he was left to ponder where it had gone. So he feigned losing his glasses to cover up his actions and to buy more time. You may recall, Jack, that he searched his hips and his waist and even his pants, but never his shirt, or the top of his head where most people place their glasses. Who searches for glasses on their waistline?"

Enzo shook his head. "Later I realized that the imposter who had been looking for his glasses was punching in the codes for the safe on a tiny alpha-numeric pad. How could he see those small letters and numbers if he needed glasses?

"When he said he was going to place the coin in the safe, he actually meant to get the gun; he had finally realized where it was. He nearly killed us."

Detective Borkowski looked over his notes while three big officers restrained Armando Sutter. It was growing dark outside.

Enzo inspected all the crates the police officers had opened. He gazed in my direction, then came over, pushed me aside, and stuck the crowbar into the weathered crate on which I had been sitting. Enzo pressed all his weight onto it and it creaked open.

Inside the crate, a shirtless, portly man with short white hair and beard sat up. He was bound and gagged, and his bloody chest had been scored repeatedly with something sharp.

Enzo cut the man free. "I'm guessing Sutter used his hunting knife to maim you, Mr. Marshall. I'm sorry I wasn't at my best today. I should've known he was an imposter."

"Emily…is she okay?" asked the real James Marshall. He was barely able to speak. "That Sutter…he started torturing me this morning until I gave him…codes…didn't want him to hurt Emily."

"It's all right, Mr. Marshall," said Enzo.

One of the paramedics gave Marshall an injection of pain killers.

"The thumping noise we heard was you trying to warn us," said Enzo.

"I was," said Marshall, "too weak to do anything, but had energy to kick the crate." Emily came into the room and threw her hands around her father.

Enzo turned to the detective. "Because Emily involved the police and me in this, Sutter's situation became urgent enough to change plans; he would torture Marshall to get the codes to open the safe, as opposed to laborious hours of safe-cracking."

The paramedics had Armando Sutter on a gurney, ready to take him away. Enzo looked dismayed. He went to the wretched man and asked, "Why, Sutter? A man like you would know the value of this treasure years beforehand. So why didn't you come to steal it years earlier? Why now? What is the urgency?"

Armando Sutter coughed, shaking the I.V. tubes attached to his arms.

Enzo's eyes widened. "I should have known. From your emaciated look and pallor, and that cough. You don't have much time left, do you?"

The scarecrow on the gurney looked away.

"But why the treasure?" insisted Enzo. "What good is money to you—unless—the man with the burned face!"

"For my son," said Sutter. His voice was muffled by deep breathing. The paramedics dressed his wound. "When he was a boy, he came into my lab. He was a curious boy. The acid was an accident. It disfigured him for life. I did all this for my son. He hasn't been able to do anything worthwhile in life with that burned body…that pink face…and those eyes. The least I could do was set him up with a fortune."

A young officer appeared at the door and called to Detective Borkowski. "Detective, we caught an armed man. He was approaching the house through the woods. His face looks awful, sir."

Borkowski leaned over Sutter's bandaged face and said, "Looks like you and your son will spend a long time in prison."

Sutter coughed again. "The cancer will kill me in less than a month," he said with a woeful gaze. "I wanted to leave something for my son. But now I've condemned him." The scarecrow man gazed at Emily and James Marshall, embraced in a hug. Sutter's eyes welled with tears as the paramedics took him away.

Enzo called his wife. He then led me outside into the cool autumn evening. "Hurry up, Jack," said Enzo. "We have to get back to the train station. My son still has a burning fever."

THE CASE OF VAMBERRY THE WINE MERCHANT

by Jack Grochot

Our visitor at Baker Street this crisp, sunny autumn afternoon was overcome with anxiety, pacing back and forth in front of the settee and, alternately, seating himself on it momentarily, then rising to pace once more. "My dilemma," he said with agitation to my friend Sherlock Holmes, "is profound. If I act to engage your services, Mr Holmes, it could mean her death. But if I do nothing, her life is nonetheless in danger."

Holmes sat speechless, his bony elbows resting on the arms of the chair, his slender fingertips touched together, and his dark eyes vacant. He waited patiently for Bascomb McHugh to complete his laboured thoughts. After an elongated silence, McHugh blurted out: "Damn! It's your advice that I need this instant. Can I pay you for that alone? I must find a way out of this predicament and protect my sweet little sister."

As he had explained earlier, McHugh found himself in the midst of a problem that had no simple answer, and the fate of his kidnapped sister hung in the balance. She was married to Heathcliff Vamberry, a wine merchant in the Hampshire countryside west of London, and upon a visit there the day before, a Sunday, McHugh learned that the petite and comely woman was missing from her home. He questioned his brother-in-law harshly, for the two never got along, and finally came to find out that Mrs Vamberry had been abducted while alone in her house adjacent to the winery as her husband was tending to his vineyard. Vamberry discovered a ransom note, pasted together with letters and words cut out from a newspaper, on the dining room table. He reluctantly showed it to McHugh. It demanded fifty thousand pounds for Mrs Vamberry's safe return, and it warned in bold letters:

"No coppers, else she dies."

The crude communication instructed the husband to leave the money in a canvas sack on a bridge over the River Avon about two kilometers from the winery on Tuesday night at ten o'clock.

"And here it is, Mr Holmes," Bascomb McHugh stated, "late in the day on Monday, and my brother-in-law has gone to the bank to withdraw his savings, which amounts to a sum of around thirty thousand pounds. I am well fixed, and I can lend him the remainder, but what guarantee do we have that my poor, beautiful sister will be unharmed?" His icy blue eyes flashed, anticipating the worst outcome. It was at this point that McHugh emphasised his profound dilemma and begged Holmes for advice.

Holmes rose and approached the mantle to retrieve a cherrywood pipe half full of shag tobacco. Ever calm in stressful situations, he contemplated briefly while he nonchalantly struck a match and inhaled the mixture. "Advice I can offer free of charge," he told McHugh, adding: "If I were Mr Vamberry, I would send someone such as yourself to the authorities—rather than go himself, for he might be under surveillance—and allow the police to become involved, because they are experienced in delicate matters that require discreet maneuvering. If this is what he and you decide, there is no need for my involvement whatsoever."

Sounding disappointed, McHugh exchanged farewells with Holmes and me, donned his well-brushed top hat, straightened his black silk waistcoat, smoothed the wrinkles out of his grey Harris-tweed trousers, glanced at the pocket watch on the end of a gold Albert chain, and went down the hallway steps with erect bearing toward a waiting brougham. That he was prosperous was of no doubt, but that he was a London barrister was evident only to Holmes when McHugh entered our flat.

"He seemed shocked, Watson," observed Holmes, "that I knew his occupation, especially when I explained that it was a peculiarity of mine to surmise one's means of a livelihood merely by appearances. If truth be known, the not-too- infrequent mention of his name in the dailies for passionately winning acquittals against Scotland Yard's most competent inspectors gave him away when he arrived. Perhaps now that he is so close to the victims of a crime he'll have a different opinion of the miscreants he represents and the necessity for justice. In any event, if I am not mistaken, I believe we shall see Mr McHugh again, and soon."

That evening, Holmes and I dined at home after Mrs Hudson, our landlady, surprised us with a supper of smoked pork chops, scalloped potatoes, and a fresh spinach salad. Afterward, we walked leisurely to the Strand for a copy of the evening *Globe* and shared it by the crackling fireplace, commenting to each other about the articles we determined to be of notable interest. "Here is a man after my own heart, Watson," murmured Holmes when reading a feature story. "He has taken up beekeeping in retirement and earns as much as he did as a groom by selling honey to London grocers and village neighbours."

"The work is not as light as one would imagine, Holmes," I countered, "and in the winter there is no profit."

"All the same, the lifestyle is appealing," Holmes noted, then folded the newspaper onto the armchair next to mine and began to busy himself at the deal-topped table, where he was in the middle of an experiment that required a dash of sugar and a splash of white vinegar to disguise the taste of the poison he was concocting.

"It is colourless and odourless, right where I want it, Watson," he intoned. "Now all we need do is capture a rat behind the Chinese restaurant around the corner to test how deadly my formula can be. That it is lethal I have no worries, but the trick will be to see if it can be detected in the blood or in the organs. The result will be the subject of my next monograph."

I was in no frame of mind to go out and trap a rat, so I retired for the night, but Holmes fashioned a box out of some loose cardboard under the table and left the apartment.

In the morning, the box was sitting on top of the table and the small beast inside was stiff as a board. Before breakfast, Holmes occupied himself dissecting the unfortunate creature and examining the innards under a microscope. After we ate, we spent the rest of the forenoon on a trip to the Great Peter Street library, where Holmes researched articles and books in preparation for his writing the monograph, while I perused *The Daily Telegraph*, *The Guardian*, and *The Morning Chronicle*, finding very little in them to be noteworthy. On the way back to Baker Street, we spoke at length about McHugh's problem and wondered if Mrs Vamberry was still alive. "Tomorrow we shall hear from him if all is not resolved tonight," Holmes conjectured. "Kidnappings usually end miserably, despite the best efforts of the official police."

At about one o'clock on Wednesday, McHugh's carriage pulled up in front of our building, and he alighted, along with a companion, both looking sombre. As I watched from the window and described their arrival to Holmes, he put down his pen on the desk where he had been writing. "It appears last night and this morning didn't go well," he assumed. "I would hazard a guess that Mr McHugh has brought Mr Vamberry and they will want me to locate Mrs Vamberry in perfect health."

We heard Mrs Hudson's footsteps on the stairs a minute or so after the door bell had rung, and she came in to announce that McHugh and Vamberry were anxious to see Holmes immediately. "It's about the missing woman that Mr McHugh spoke of the day before yesterday," Mrs Hudson said. "The man with him is her husband. They are both very distraught."

"Send them up at once, then," Holmes directed, and thanked her for the warning. "You may leave the door open," he said as he slipped into his green double-breasted jacket and buttoned it.

In an instant, McHugh was standing on the threshold, with Vamberry meekly behind him. McHugh waved his index finger at Holmes, as if making a point to a jury in a tense courtroom, chastising Holmes for giving poor advice. "We did as you suggested and contacted the Hampshire district's special constable, who proceeded to make a horrible and thorough mess of an already disastrous situation," McHugh began. "Our Phoebe is still unaccounted for and the ransom money is gone."

"Give me the precise details of your experience, calmly," Holmes answered unapologetically while casually offering the two guests the armchairs with his outstretched hand.

They accepted his invitation and McHugh continued the narrative:

"When I left here Monday, I drove straight to the winery and persuaded my brother-in-law to seek the assistance of the authorities. After a hurried meal, I then rode to the police station late in the evening, and waited an interminable time for the officer on duty to fetch the special constable Isaac Thornburgh from his home, where he was found in his bed-clothes.

"He listened to my story and decided to ensnare one of the kidnappers on the bridge when he came to pick up the canvas sack. Thornburgh said he would then convince the offender that it was in his best interest to lead the police to where his accomplices had secreted Mrs Vamberry, because there was no escaping the gallows if she were to be killed.

"I was reticent to go along with Thornburgh's plan, thinking my sister would have a better chance of survival if Mr Vamberry and I simply followed the instructions in the ransom note. However, Thornburgh explained that the authorities would act to intercept the transfer of money and rescue my sister regardless of my opinion, so I acceded to his wishes.

"Yesterday morning, I was committed to representing a client scheduled for a judicial hearing, so I went to the Central Criminal Court and later to the bank to withdraw the twenty thousand pounds that would complete the ransom package, just as Thornburgh had stipulated. I then returned to the winery, where my brother-in-law placed the funds in his safe with the thirty thousand pounds he had secured from his accounts."

Throughout McHugh's recital, Vamberry sat without uttering a word, nodding in agreement as McHugh went on:

"The rest of the day passed slowly, with hardly any conversation, except a word here and there about how much Phoebe means to each of us. A half hour before ten o'clock we took the canvas sack to my brougham and drove together to the bridge. Heathcliff here placed the sack on the walkway in the middle of the structure. Thornburgh already had positioned his men in the bushes at either end of the bridge so they could have a view of the sack from both directions.

"But to our chagrin, because of the season a dense fog settled in over the river and obscured their sight. It was a pea-souper, so thick the police were unable even to see the bridge.

"I expected to return to the winery in the morning to find our Phoebe alive and well, but instead, only my brother-in-law was there with Thornburgh, who reported that the canvas sack had disappeared during the night without the police hearing or seeing anything at all. They have bungled this affair royally, and you, Mr Holmes, are our last hope to bring my sister home safely."

Vamberry then chimed in, speaking sheepishly. He nervously scratched his bald head and stroked his clean-shaven chin and cheeks. "My wife, Mr Holmes, is of paramount concern to me, but the loss of the money has wiped me out. My vineyard is in ruin because of the phylloxera epidemic that has spread from France to Britain, and so my business is failing for lack of good wine to sell. If you could recover the ransom as well as save Phoebe's life, I would be eternally grateful."

Holmes said nothing for a short time, slowly walking about the room with his hands clasped behind his back, then: "I fear the worst for Mrs Vamberry, so if I involve myself in your case, you might come to learn that I have discovered the identity of the kidnappers without having achieved her return unharmed. As for the ransom, there is a fifty-fifty chance of success."

"Oh, I beg you to try your best, come what may," McHugh implored humbly.

"Please do," Vamberry added plaintively.

Holmes agreed to take up their cause, but first asked a question that seemed out of context. "From what banks did you obtain the ransom money?" he wanted to know.

"What has that to do with your inquiry?" Vamberry retorted.

"It might very well be that someone at one of the banks was aware of what assets you had available and conjured up the scheme to relieve you of them," Holmes told him.

"I withdrew the funds from the National Bank of England," McHugh revealed, and Vamberry named Forsythe & Company at Newmarket Heath.

With that, Holmes bade our visitors goodbye and mentioned a word of encouragement. "Possibly by the time you reach the winery Mrs Vamberry will be awaiting you at home. Do not lose hope for her." He also said he would see them in a day or so in Hampshire, "for I shall begin my investigation in London and proceed to the outskirts in due course."

After they had departed, Holmes volunteered that the matter was particularly perplexing because there was scant physical evidence upon which to rely. He didn't rule out the potential that Mrs Vamberry was unhappy in her marriage and had arranged for her own disappearance, as well as for the opportunity to flee with a tidy sum. "There is one other possibility, but it is too premature to theorise," he said cryptically, without explaining further.

Holmes excused himself and went up to his bedroom to change into his back-alley uniform, a shabby turtle-neck shirt, brown dungarees, and a lint-marked sweater. "We have time before dinner for me to consult my informants to see if they have noticed any ne'er-do-wells spending an exorbitant amount of cash that could be part of the ransom money—if indeed it is in circulation," he remarked as he hustled toward the stairwell.

I had a need for some fresh air myself, so I donned my derby and grabbed my walking stick for a pleasant jaunt around the park. I noticed geese on the pond, an indication that the coming winter was still a month or more away, but the gathering clouds were a sign of impending rain, so I hurried back to 221-B before I got a good soaking. I had been gone for about two hours, but Holmes remained out on his excursion. He came through the doorway at nearly six o'clock and was in a talkative mood.

"All the known hoodlums are as poor as church mice," he proclaimed, "except for Archie Stamford, the forger, who recently inherited ten thousand pounds from his dear mother, a forever tolerant woman who bailed him out of trouble a number of times when she was vibrant. Her generosity was for certain an inducement for Archie to continue his criminal behaviour. She saw it differently, though, as only a devoted mother could."

Holmes changed into his more dignified clothes and we ate pasta with shrimp and scallops at Carbone's Italian Restaurant on Miles Street, sharing a carafe of Chianti while Holmes plotted his next move. "I shall make inquiries at the two banks and develop a better picture of this complicated puzzle," he postulated, then turned the conversation to the repercussions of the phylloxera plague, the performance of Genevieve Masters in a drama we attended at the Lyceum Theatre, and the effects on society in the future with the advent of electric lights.

No sooner than Holmes had left Thursday morning, Bascomb McHugh and Heathcliff Vamberry arrived to bring him an urgent request. They refused to wait for Holmes to get back, saying only that they wanted him to cease his investigation immediately. They asked me to convey the message because it was a matter of life and death for Mrs Vamberry. I told them I would relay the information but that Holmes would want to know why they were so intent upon removing him from the case.

"We shall return this afternoon with the explanation, but by all means do not allow Mr Holmes to proceed," McHugh demanded before he abruptly turned and marched down the stairs in a rush, Vamberry following briskly to keep up.

I was perplexed by the sudden change of attitude, and I expressed my misgivings to Holmes when he came through the door about an hour after lunchtime. "Curious," he said, "although it is consistent with what I have determined thus far." He didn't go into detail; rather, he mumbled something about Mrs Hudson's kindness and made a sandwich with the leftover slices of roast beef and horseradish she had brought up for us earlier.

It was nearly three-thirty before McHugh and Vamberry passed through our doorway to confront Holmes standing at the sitting-room window, looking out at the endless parade of pedestrians and horse-drawn traffic. "I understand you gentlemen wish me to disengage myself from your service," he offered as a greeting, with his straight and narrow back still toward them.

"It is imperative that you do so," McHugh affirmed. "You see, Mr Holmes, we have been alerted by the kidnappers that if you persist, our Phoebe will be destroyed." He shoved a sheet of paper under Holmes's hawk-like nose as Holmes turned to face them.

The note contained more pasted words and letters cut out from a newspaper.

"We told you no coppers, and that includes Holmes," the first line read.

"I found this today attached to my front door with a dagger," Vamberry interjected, pointing a quivering finger at the sheet of paper.

"Unless you were followed to my address, there is no way anyone could have known of my entanglement in your concern," Holmes insisted.

"That is immaterial, Mr Holmes," Bascomb McHugh continued, "because the fact is they do know, and we must obey their instructions for Phoebe's sake."

Holmes took the note from McHugh and scanned the entire contents. It ordered Vamberry to place another fifty thousand pounds on the walkway of the bridge at ten o'clock that night. "And come alone this time," it warned.

"I am going to take it myself and catch whoever comes to retrieve it," McHugh advised. "I'll make him tell where they've hidden my sister, by God."

"You are making a foolish mistake," said Holmes, objecting, "but you are my client, and I cannot go contrary to your desires."

"Bascomb and I disagree on most issues," Vamberry said boldly, to conclude the conversation, "but not on this. He will accomplish what you and the police were unable to."

After they were gone, Holmes sank into one of his reveries, stretching out on the sofa and plunking the strings of his violin with melancholy refrains. He declined my invitation to buy his dinner at Simpson's, saying he had no appetite, so I walked to the establishment alone and found him still on the sofa in the doldrums when I returned. "Look here, Holmes," I scolded, "it is not a failure of your professional status to be dismissed from the employment of a fool and his relative."

"No, but it is a setback, especially since I was on the verge of a breakthrough," he responded.

Holmes's depression continued into the next afternoon until a development shook us to the core. I hastily entered our rooms, huffing and puffing from a trip to the newsstand for a copy of *The Daily Gazette*. The headline on the front page of the Friday evening edition screamed out about the violent death of McHugh.

"A Singular Tragedy," it read, and below it: "Prominent Lawyer Slain on Bridge in Hampshire."

The accompanying story revealed that Bascomb McHugh had been stabbed repeatedly in the chest and throat, his body having been discovered slouched on the seat of his carriage by a brother-in-law, Heathcliff Vamberry, late the night before. The article did not specify why McHugh was crossing the river at such an hour, or why he was in Hampshire instead of at home in London. Special Constable Isaac Thornburgh was quoted as saying the police were following up undisclosed leads and suspected a gangster was responsible for the murder. Constable Thornburgh mentioned nothing of the kidnapping of Phoebe Vamberry or the fifty thousand pounds McHugh was carrying. The special constable merely told the reporter that robbery appeared to be the motive for the vicious attack.

"Such is the consequence when an amateur takes matters into his own hands," Holmes commented with coolness after reading the account. "I have an obligation to my client now to find a solution to this grisly mystery. If the killing of Mr McHugh is solved, so will be the case of his sister."

Holmes was still in his mouse-coloured dressing-gown, so he quickly changed to his traveling clothes and soon we were on an Underground train to Oxford Circus Station on the far western edge of London, connecting there to a rented surrey at a livery stable, then into picturesque and affluent Hampshire County. Holmes rode with his tight-fitting cloth cap pulled down over his bushy eyebrows as we went past one stately stone house after another, with well-manicured lawns and impeccable flower gardens, then a polo field with players and ponies making practice runs, and lastly a patch of woods where a wild boar stood munching acorns—until we halted finally at the constabulary headquarters to meet Special Constable Thornburgh.

He was a short, thin man of about thirty-five years in age, with a thick black moustache that matched his wavy hair.

"I have heard of your participation in some of Scotland Yard's investigations, Mr Holmes," he said by way of introduction, "but there is nothing you can contribute to this one. We have several suspects in mind and are narrowing the field through the process of elimination." He spoke with confidence and authority, his pointy chin and wide-set grey eyes aiming toward the ceiling in a gesture of aloofness. Holmes, not offended, nonetheless offered his assistance and asked for some details of the crime scene.

"Mr Vamberry discovered the blood-soaked body on the seat of Mr McHugh's brougham, his hands holding the reins in a death grip and his face contorted, as if surprised," Constable Thornburgh disclosed. "Mr Vamberry told us that he anxiously waited at home for his brother-in-law to return from his mission, but when Mr McHugh failed to appear by two o'clock in the morning, Mr Vamberry walked toward the bridge. He went along the same route the brougham would have taken, hoping he would encounter Mr McHugh on the way. Mr Vamberry reached the bridge and saw the carriage in the middle, his brother-in-law obviously dead, and the money sack gone. It won't be but a day or so before we have the perpetrators locked up and learn the whereabouts of Mrs Vamberry."

Holmes then posed a rhetorical question: "Does not the position of the corpse with its multiple wounds suggest a direction different from your theory?"

"What do you mean by that—do you have a better one?" the officer shot back, glaring at Holmes with irritation.

"I shall pursue other avenues and concentrate on my direction, then I shall reveal all when I have reached a conclusion," Holmes answered ambiguously before walking away. "His demeanour reminds me of Inspector Lestrade's," Holmes confided to me in private as we climbed into the surrey, referring to the beady-eyed Scotland Yard official who usually was obstinate after crossing paths with the empire's only indefatigable consulting detective.

We drove toward the bridge above the River Avon after first asking guidance to its location from a woman strolling with her clipped and trimmed French poodle. "Be vigilant," she cautioned, "it is a dangerous place for such a peaceful neighborhood—there was a robbery and murder there just yesterday."

At the bridge, Holmes scrupulously examined the surrounding areas on both sides, determining that a footpath at either end could have concealed a person from the police hiding in the bushes along the road in the dense fog Tuesday night. "They expected a con-veyance and neglected to cover the more devious approach," he gathered. "Come, Watson, there is nothing more to see here. Let us pay a visit to Mr Vamberry."

We gained information from another passerby on how to best reach the winery, which was twenty minutes away. It was set back from the road almost out of view, with tall oak and elm trees lining the circular drive. Halfway along, we glimpsed a sprawling stucco and brick structure of two stories with bay windows on both levels. At the far end was a small grassy plot with a walkway paved by cobblestones leading to the residence. Behind the well-appointed brick home was a vast vineyard of at least ten hectares, showing mostly stems practically bare of leaves or grapes.

Sherlock Holmes led the way through the main entrance to the winery, which was absent of any aroma one might expect—due to the lack of production. The walls were covered with bottles on racks, the majority of the stock bearing labels from California and New York in the United States, plus from La Rioja in Spain, and the upper banks of the Douro River in Portugal. In a larger adjoining room were huge vats, empty presses, and row after row of barrels stacked on their sides. Holmes studied the collection, sniffed the rims of some, and scraped from one a residue of a white powdery substance into a vial he carried in a leather case in his jacket pocket.

There was no sign of Vamberry, so Holmes beckoned me to follow him to locate the proprietor. Just as we reached the exit, Vamberry stepped out of the privy at the corner of the building and gave a start.

"Mr Holmes! What are you doing here?" he demanded.

"We came to buy a bottle of wine for our table this evening," Holmes answered coyly. "And to make inquiries into the death of my client, Bascomb McHugh."

"But you were removed from our case," Vamberry replied, impatient, it seemed, to see us leave.

"That was prior to his demise," Holmes contradicted. "I have since re-engaged myself, apparently not to your liking."

"I should think the police are handling matters satisfactorily, and your involvement is totally unnecessary," Vamberry shouted, strutting past us and through the door to conclude the discussion.

Undeterred, Holmes followed him in, I at his heels.

"I believe a medium-bodied dry white would do nicely," Holmes continued. "Which do you recommend?"

"What?" Vamberry sputtered with an edge to his voice.

"For our table tonight," Holmes responded in a friendly manner.

"Oh, but of course, you came for a bottle of wine, as you said," Vamberry remarked, losing his combative posture. "I would choose the Vidal Blanc from a California vineyard—two sovereigns and four shillings, a bit pricey, but that's because it is imported." He escorted Holmes to the appropriate rack and raised the label for him to read.

Holmes nodded in approval and paid the man.

We left and headed for the livery stable to return the horse and buggy. On the way, Holmes said he found it odd that Vamberry had failed to bring up the topic of his missing spouse. "Out of sight, out of mind, I suppose," Holmes commented wistfully, twirling his hand above his cranium.

Once we were back at Baker Street, Holmes was eager to analyse the white powdery substance to determine its chemical composition. He arranged his assortment of liquid compounds on the deal-topped table and began his experiments. "I have only a minute sample of the residue, so I must make every test count," he noted with a serious expression as he ignited the Bunsen lamp. "I shall start with the presumption that the substance is potassium hydroxide."

"Lye?" I exclaimed, looking up from a copy of *The Echo* I had procured from a vendor on our way home. "Mr Vamberry or his wife must have used a perfectly aged wine barrel to make soap, of all things."

"Or perhaps something sinister," Holmes guessed. He tinkered with several decanters for about an hour, saying nary a word, then he cried loudly: "It is so! We haven't a second to waste, my good man. Get your hat and coat—we're about to roust Constable Thornburgh out of his bed-clothes for the second time this week."

Without protest, I complied with anticipation, for I knew the climax of Holmes's investigation was not far off. In the darkness, through patches of fog, we made our way to the Underground and were aboard the night-express to the far West End for another foray into Hampshire. We awakened the manager of the livery stable and hired another carriage that would take us to the constabulary head-quarters. There, Holmes stunned the officer in charge by declaring he had crucial evidence in the homicide of McHugh and the death of Mrs Vamberry.

"The death of Mrs Vamberry?" the officer challenged. "You say she's dead, do you? Well, we have a suspect in custody who can lead us to her alive, mister."

"May I speak with him?" Holmes implored.

"Not without the permission of Constable Thornburgh, and I'm not disturbing him in bed again," the officer contended, his voice raised. "You'll have to wait until morning. He'll be here at eight o'clock sharp."

The officer was unrelenting, even when Holmes argued that morning might be too late.

"Here! Here! What's all this fuss about?" came another booming voice from across the squad room. It belonged to Special Constable Isaac Thornburgh, who, as it turned out, had been unable to sleep, thinking that his prisoner might have had a change of heart and decided to come clean about the whereabouts of Mrs

Vamberry. Constable Thornburgh addressed the officer in charge, sarcastically:

"McGee, this is no way to treat Scotland Yard's most indispensible assistant. Mr Sherlock Holmes has come all the way from the city at an ungodly hour to lecture us on how to proceed." He turned to Holmes and bowed with a flair in mock respect. "Tell us, Mr Holmes, what have we done to get it wrong?"

Holmes contained his anger admirably and informed the special constable that the man in custody was not guilty of a kidnapping.

Constable Thornburgh laughed. "But we have incontrovertible evidence, you see. He was in possession of a diamond-studded brooch that Mrs Vamberry was wearing the day she was abducted. Dan Fullen, a common thief until he joined a higher class of criminals, tried to sell the brooch to a pawn broker in Winchester. We had circulated a description of Mrs Vamberry's jewelry to all the merchants and were notified when Fullen attempted to turn the brooch into cash. We apprehended him red-handed, so to speak. He denied any knowledge of Mrs Vamberry, but now we are waiting for him to sing a different tune."

"What tune did he sing when you arrested him?" Holmes wanted to learn.

"Oh, he claimed to have snatched the brooch off the blouse of an elderly woman shopping at Berkeley Square in London," Constable Thornburgh related, shaking his head and clucking.

"Have you made an effort to verify or discredit his story?" Holmes asked, adding: "Scotland Yard surely would have a report—I presume the woman exists—and she could easily identify this scoundrel Fullen, as well as the brooch he stole."

"There is no need, Mr Holmes. Heathcliff Vamberry has confirmed that the brooch belongs to his wife," Constable Thornburgh insisted.

"And what if Dan Fullen is not the prevaricator, only a strong-arm robber?" queried Holmes, a question which Constable Thornburgh greeted with disbelief.

"There is another way to make certain who is telling the truth," Holmes continued. "Accompany Dr Watson and me to the winery tonight. There is no time to lose."

Constable Thornburgh resisted, saying it was too late at night and that if Holmes were off-course with his hunch, the wine maker would be justifiably resentful of the police because of the unwarranted intrusion.

"Then follow us there and stay in the background," Holmes proposed. "Dr Watson and I will confront Mr Vamberry alone." This the special constable found acceptable, and we departed at once.

We arrived to find the winery and house in pitch darkness, and there was no response when Holmes banged the knocker on the front door of the residence. We were about to leave when Holmes stepped to the rear of the building. "Come here, Watson, and tell me what you see," he cajoled, pointing into the vastness of the vineyard. To my surprise, there was the glow of a lantern off in the distance.

"Tell Constable Thornburgh to join us this instant, for we are in the nick of time to witness the completion of the crime," Holmes ordered. I walked quickly to the end of the drive and persuaded the special constable to follow me to where Holmes stood vigil.

We moved stealthily along the rows between the bare vines toward the stationary light. "Quietly, now," Holmes whispered as we drew nearer. When we got to within ten paces of the lantern, we watched in amazement as Heathcliff Vamberry worked with a digging iron and shovel to enlarge a hole for the barrel that sat on a wheelbarrow behind him.

"The bereaved husband is preparing to lay his beloved wife to rest, in peace," Holmes bellowed, sending the man slumping to his knees.

"Oh, Lord, forgive me for what I have done," he moaned. "She was an abominable nag, always wanting more than I could provide, but I loved her so. I only meant to silence her—yet my grip on her neck was too strong and she died in my arms, her beautiful brown eyes open. How did you know, Mr Holmes?"

"I suspected you almost from the start, Mr Vamberry," Holmes told him. "When I learned at your bank that you had not, in fact, withdrawn thirty thousand pounds for your wife's ransom, I deduced that you had constructed the first bogus note from the kidnappers as a ruse to cover your tracks and to defraud your brother-in-law of a part of his fortune. Every turn of events after that merely defined my theory. And today I also discovered this barrel, and I noticed where you had spilled the lye in your effort to hasten the decomposition of the remains and mask a tell-tale odour."

"Please get up off your knees, Mr Vamberry," Constable Thornburgh requested, holding out a pair of handcuffs.

Vamberry, still shaken, leaned on the wheelbarrow for balance and accidentally tipped it over, hurling the barrel onto the ground with a terrible impact, which caused the lid to break apart. To our horror, the head and shoulders of an emaciated, tiny woman landed in the shallow grave.

"Oh, my precious Phoebe," Vamberry lamented.

Constable Thornburgh clasped Vamberry's wrists in the handcuffs and we strode without speaking toward our vehicles. When we reached the winery, Holmes stopped and wondered aloud if Vamberry wanted to make a clean breast of the entire affair. "Since there were no kidnappers," said Holmes dryly, "would you care to tell us how you killed Bascomb McHugh?"

"But I didn't—" Vamberry began to say.

Holmes interrupted him in mid-sentence. "If you would unlock your safe, it will prove your innocence."

"The money is all there—seventy thousand pounds, twenty thousand from the first night on the bridge, and fifty thousand from the second," Vamberry confessed. "He was an interfering, arrogant buffoon and I hated every bone in his body."

"It was an obvious crime of passion," Holmes explained to Constable Thornburgh, "because of the numerous mortal wounds. That the victim was seated in the brougham, and not slain on the deck of the bridge while fighting off an attacker, led me to conclude that the murder was committed by a passenger on his right. The killer could only have been his confederate in the delivery of the ransom money."

"What becomes of me now?" Vamberry asked, overwrought, his head drooped in a display of contrition.

"If I have anything to say about it, I'll see you get a short drop at the Old Bailey," Constable Thornburgh answered venomously. "As for you," he said proudly, turning to Sherlock Holmes, "I shall make mention of your assisting the police when I meet with the press in the morning to announce that I have solved two murders at one time."

✗

UP TO NO GOOD

by Laird Long

It was a busy night at the old hotel, two guests checking out permanently …

I was the outside woman, stationed in the lobby behind a newspaper to keep track of any unusual comings and goings. While my partner in the PI biz, Reg Wyant, was the inside man, up in Tommy O'Halloran's room on the seventh floor of the old brownstone residential hotel.

Tommy O'Halloran was Ma Bennigan's kept man, her intimate friend outside of marriage. There was a brewing war between the four major factions that controlled the city's underworld, and Ma didn't want any collateral harm coming to her loved one. So she'd hired Reg and I to act as bodyguards/watchdogs for the sveltely-built O'Halloran.

It was a nice, easy assignment the first day and night. The following night, things went a little sideways.

I was ensconced in one of the armchairs in the lobby, when I eyeballed Tess Orlov flouncing through the front doors of the hotel. Tess was the mistress of the head of one of the other crime families, as beautiful as Tommy was handsome.

I watched her sashay over to the ancient elevator, press the button. Surprised and suspicious as I was at her appearance, I still wished her luck, knowing from frustrated personal experience that that particular lift, an old cage model, was as slow as molasses in January. And it was January.

Tess waited and waited, glancing at her watch, before the feeble bell finally dinged and she pushed the grate open, stepped inside, shut the grate and slowly rose. At 9:15.

She was back down and out of the elevator at 9:30. Just missing Julie Deng by a minute or so. Julie was a ranking lieutenant in another crime family. She slipped through the hotel front doors and sailed up the stairs at the rear of the lobby.

I lost interest in the news of the day in the paper, as I tried to figure out the current events here and now. But I had little time for the skull-session, before Julie Deng was back down the stairs and out the doors. At 9:35.

My gut senses really churned when Sollie DiPietro lumbered into the lobby not five minutes after Julie had left. Sollie was a well-known collector/enforcer with the fourth largest crime family that fed in the city's underbelly. He hit the elevator button and stood there, scowling. Then he rabbit-punched the button for action.

He went up at 9:40, came down at 9:45—via the stairs.

It was too much coincidence for one evening. I beeped my partner's number on my cellphone. No answer. I buzzed Tommy O'Halloran's room phone. Ditto. I climbed the stairs up to the seventh floor three at a time.

My partner and Ma Bennigan's lover were as dead as Jimmy Hoffa up in Room 705. A silencer-equipped .32 lay on the floor next to their bodies.

I could've called the cops, should've called Ma Bennigan. But I knew my tuchus was on the line if I didn't at least round up the murderer, and quick. So I gathered together Tess Orlov, Julie Deng, and Sollie DiPietro in my office for a chinwag. My .38 and I chaired the meeting.

"Why did you pay Tommy O'Halloran a visit tonight, Tess?"

"I—I just wanted to introduce myself, compare... notes, sort of."

I grunted, swivelled my gun and gaze over to Julie. "And you?"

"I was authorized to offer Tommy a deal—to provide information to our organization."

I snorted, shook down Sollie with my personality and persuader.

"I was supposed to collect some gambling debts the guy owed one of our operators."

I groaned. I didn't have all night, perhaps many more nights. "Any of you been to Tommy's hotel before tonight, up to his room?"

All three shook their heads, solemnly innocent as could be.

I grinned. Then levelled an accusing steel barrel stare at the murderer. "Ever meet Ma Bennigan before?" I asked the guilty party.

Julie Deng coolly regarded me and my gun, not about to confess to the murder of Tommy O'Halloran and Reg Wyant on my say-so.

I spilled the beans to her and the others. "All three of you claimed you'd never been to Tommy O'Halloran's hotel before, yet Julie here used the stairs to get up to his room on the seventh floor—as if she knew the ancient elevator would slow down any quick entrance and exit. Like she'd been there before, to case the set-up for the whack job."

The other two faded out of the picture. Leaving me and Julie. And Ma made three.

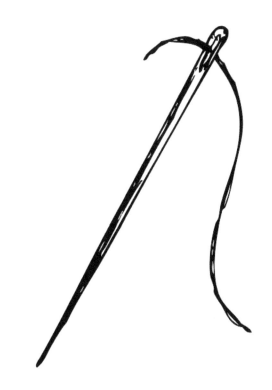

"Wrong needle Watson!"

WE'RE UPSIDE DOWN AND INSIDE OUT

By Jay Carey

The house looked as if it had exploded. The four walls had fallen open, flat against the ground. On them, instead of shingles or siding, you saw curled wallpaper and accordioned blinds. Pieces of the roof were scattered nearby.

This was what happened when hurricane winds broke a window. The storm got inside the house and lifted the roof the way air lifts the wing of a plane. Then it was tossed aside.

Detective Eureka Kilburn had seen a lot of hurricane wreckage in the past decade. By 2048 she was used to the bizarre post-storm landscape: bright sunlight over broken foliage, shattered white wood, and earth so wet it was like walking on a sponge. But sometimes even Eureka marveled at the different ways that high winds could destroy things.

There was a curious beauty to the scene. The water in the lawn reflected the shimmering heavens so it looked as if grass was growing up through a bright shining sky.

She was here on Tangerine Drive because shortly before the storm someone claimed to have seen a man featured on one of the "CrimeWatch" program cycles. They played these things monthly till the person was caught, and sometimes the cycle seemed to go on forever. Thanks to the chaos created by rising sea levels, Florida had become a haven of sorts for criminals and deadbeats. Mostly, the residents of Sarasota left them alone. But the screen had a powerful allure. It conferred glamour on turning a man in.

The sighting was unusually credible because the wanted man, named Nat Serpas, had once lived in the neighborhood where he was spotted. It made sense that he would return to his old haunts. Years ago, when he was in his twenties, he'd used phony credit card numbers "by mistake." Now he was wanted in Atlanta for tricking a 72-year old woman out of her life savings, just the sort of larger career he'd been heading for.

Det. Kilburn exited the squad car with caution. From the road, the house looked as if all its secrets had been exposed. But it was peeled open the way a magician can make a trick box collapse to display its deceptive emptiness. Next thing you know, a pigeon is flying out or a goldfish is swimming in a bowl in front of your very eyes.

The house had consisted of a single story. The inner walls were gone, and the taller furniture seemed to have ended up out in the yard. A refrigerator leaned against a palm tree. A leather sofa tilted back as if it had turned into a porch swing. A car was completely overturned, its wheels sticking up like Mickey Mouse ears. There were few cars on the road any more, so the presence of this one probably meant that someone had driven it down from the north.

As she approached the floor of the house she heard a muffled shout. And another. There was a man in the car, upside down, stuck between the front and back seats. His face was contorted, and his mouth was open. Although he was forming words, they were deadened. This was to be expected, as the windows were closed, but the sound was eerily reminiscent of a person trapped underwater. The large glittering puddles added to the effect.

He was repeating slowly and emphatically, "Get. Me. Out."

It was hard to assess his condition. His inverted position confounded the brain. His neck was curled, and the back of his head was flat against the crushed top of the car.

"Are you all right?" She exaggerated the movement of her mouth to help him read her lips.

She thought she deciphered, "Leg is broken."

Which meant he could be going into shock.

He went on to say something else at length and with increasing exasperation. She could not make it out.

This man was not Nat Serpas. He was older and heavier than Serpas, with a square, Irish face and salt-and-pepper hair so neatly trimmed it stayed smooth even upside down. He looked familiar, though, and she went back through her memory as she automatically tried the doors.

"I. Will. Get. Tools," she said finally, bending down for a good look at him. He seemed to be sensitive to her scrutiny, and the self-consciously bland control he exerted over himself as he looked back at her struck a chord. She tried to place it.

She associated him with some sort of disconnect, something more than just his topsy-turvy position. The disparity was between this particular Celtic face and the name attached to it.

Ghotikar! His name was Kevin Ghotikar, and he'd been on TV, too. Not on a "CrimeWatch" most-wanted type program like Serpas, but rather its opposite. He'd been tried and acquitted of murdering his wealthy wife on the outskirts of Charlotte a few months before. He was a banker who'd made a fortune by manipulating financial data of some sort.

During the trial his defense attorney had offered up an alternate suspect: a stranger who'd come to the house on the morning of the murder, asking if the victim had any chores he could do. When Ghotikar took the stand, he described the ensuing confrontation. He'd known immediately that the stranger was up to no good. He told him he wasn't giving out charity that day and asked why he didn't get a job for a change. In response, the stranger swore he'd come back with a gun and kill them both.

Ghotikar then chased him off the porch, threatening to call the police. He did not call them, however, because the exchange had already made him late for a meeting upon which millions of dollars depended. On the stand, when asked to describe the man, Ghotikar became agitated and cried that he would recognize him anywhere. He was in his mid-thirties, six feet two, 180 pounds, with black eyes and a black beard.

The meeting had gone well, and the money had been made, but at great cost. When Ghotikar returned home at the end of the day, he found his wife dead with a bullet through her head. "That man took her away from me!" he said.

When he left the stand, the chatter in cyberspace was that the verdict could go either way. He had spoken convincingly, but few people liked him. He was arrogant and impatient, so nothing softened the many factors against him: He was the husband, he had given a colleague a negligee for her birthday, the gun that was used had been registered in his name, and he was the only one to have seen this mysterious employment-seeking stranger. In fact, the banker was the only person who'd been proved to be at the house that day, except for the victim.

Then, at the last minute, a neighbor who'd been on a religious retreat came forward to testify that he, too, had seen a strange man at the Ghotikar's door on the day of the murder. This unknown man was tall and lean and hungry-looking. He had a scruffy beard. The neighbor had seen Ghotikar's wife Bronwyn open the door. Then he'd seen Ghotikar join her and shout at the stranger, calling him a bum. There was more shouting. But the words were indistinguishable.

On the strength of this evidence, Ghotikar was acquitted in a matter of hours. The jury members who spoke publicly said that no one doubted the testimony of the neighbor, fresh from the arms of his church. They all expressed sorrow for the banker's loss, probably because some of them were ashamed of their earlier suspicions of him. But one juror, a middle-aged woman who worked at a call center, said she thought Ghotikar might have provoked the attack on his wife. Who knew what desperate straits the bearded man was in when he'd knocked on their door?

It is possible that Ghotikar heard the same interview. After shutting himself up in the "death house" for a week, he announced angrily that he would track down the killer if it was the last thing he ever did. "You're blaming the victim!" he said, although blaming the victim's husband would have been the more accurate description. He took a leave from his job and disappeared from sight.

If Kevin Ghotikar was in Sarasota looking for the mysterious stranger, that mysterious stranger could very well be Nat Serpas. Serpas had a beard now—at least in his photo on TV. That would make two men who'd gone straight from TV to Sarasota, Florida. This place was going to get a reputation.

Eureka did not waste a lot of time looking through the squad car for an adequate substitute for "the jaws of life," which had disappeared along with most of the police force earlier in the decade. Police cars were not really equipped to deal with vehicular accidents any more. There weren't enough cars around to matter. All she could find was the chain-saw she used to clear the road. It was not large, and she didn't know how it would hold up against steel. Upon reflection, she took the silicone gloves and the jack as well.

She still didn't have anything to smash open the window with, so she decided to take a quick look through the remains of the house. It had been one of the largest in the area. Judging by the litter, there must have been plenty of stuff inside before the roof blew away. Chances were that up until the storm it had been inhabited by squatters. Anyone with the money to buy it would have fled north years ago—or maybe it had been a second home.

Now everything was in pieces, most unrecognizable. You couldn't always tell if they belonged inside or out. A lot of stuff was as wet as a marsh that shouldn't be wet at all, like the rug and the mattress. As Eureka stepped into the foyer of the house, it was like stepping into the first box of a game of hopscotch. The boundaries were more theoretical than actual. She was still surrounded by bright sunshine and she still breathed the post-hurricane air, with its peculiar and invigorating smell of ozone.

In a rectangle that delineated a former closet she found a lidless plastic bin holding a tennis racket, a baseball bat, and a cottonmouth. She managed to pick out the bat without disturbing the snake. Farther on, next to an upended oak entertainment system, was a man lying on his back: Nat Serpas. Det. Kilburn recognized his long, handsome face, his thin lips, his beard. She supposed he was hungry-looking. Most people around here were. Smashed around him were a large flat screen, several audiovisual tech modules, and half a dozen big black metal storage boxes, one of which had just missed him. He was alive, but unconscious. Det. Kilburn cuffed him in front. She wasn't unfeeling, but that was what she was there for. And if he happened to be Bronwyn Ghotikar's mysterious killer, well, he wasn't going anywhere soon.

Next Det. Kilburn went back to the car and used the baseball bat to break the right back window, which was in line with the upside-down man but not so close that he'd be hit by shards of glass.

As she was clearing the shards from the door with her gloves, he said, as clear as day, "You look like you have some initiative, thank the Lord. I've got to get out of here. What we really need is a reciprocating saw. Did you see anyone else around?" He spoke with authority, despite his breathlessness.

"First I'm going to examine you real quick." She was crouched over, her head inches from the ground, but she managed to stretch her arm far enough inside to take his pulse.

"We've no time to waste," he said sharply. "I have reason to believe there is a very dangerous man nearby."

"Dangerous?"

"It's too complicated to go into now."

"There's a man in what's left of the house, if that's what you mean," said Det. Kilburn.

"Get me my gun," he barked. "It's somewhere around here."

"He's not going to attack anyone. He's unconscious. He was almost crushed when a huge shelf fell over."

"Naturally," said Ghotikar. Bitterness overcame him. "He has the luck of the devil. Whatever he does, he gets off scot-free. He obviously didn't secure anything. But he's not the one stuck here. He's the laziest person I ever encountered. Look at that house. The roof wasn't strapped down. I've never seen such a shoddy job. Did he do anything to prepare for the storm? Put plywood over the windows, maybe? Bring his car parallel to the house? Any moron knows that's what you do." He was becoming increasingly breathless. "I didn't even grow up around here, and I can tell you that much. He's a shirker through and through." His face was turning red and blotchy. "I must keep calm!"

"You know this man?" asked Det. Klburn.

"Well enough," said Ghotikar. "He destroyed my life."

She was amazed that he had the energy to talk as much as he did.

"What are you standing around for?" he cried, as if Serpas's sloth was a contagion, and Eureka the unfortunate recipient.

This was annoying. Plus she was still not really standing. She was bent over nearly double trying to examine the door. The posture was awkward and painful for her. "I would prefer not to kill you in the process of getting you out," she said.

She turned on the chain-saw and attacked the door at the hinge. He did not flinch. She gave him that much. But the blade was not doing anything to the door except for scratching it. She was going to have to go in through the window and get at the door that way.

"Do you see my gun?" he asked.

"You don't need a gun," said Det. Kilburn.

"Yes, I do. You don't know what you're getting into here."

"I have a gun."

The banker perked up. "Yes, of course," he said. He gathered himself together and declared, "That man over there killed my wife."

"I see."

"I know it's hard to believe, but it's true. I recognized him from a TV program called 'CrimeWatch.'"

"Why didn't you call the cops? Or the TV show, for that matter?"

"The cops! They never believe a word I say. So now I have to do my own police work, too. I tell you, there is no rest for the weary."

Det. Kilburn pointed out pleasantly that eyewitness IDs were notoriously shaky.

"I looked straight at him for ten minutes, and I can read a person like that as easily as I can read the stock figures. Believe me, I have the right man."

The air was hot, but not humid. The hurricane had sucked all the moisture away. A sudden little breeze made it almost pleasant to be out doing physical labor. First she brushed the worst of the glass from the crumpled top of the car where she was going to have to sit. Then she wriggled in with the baseball bat. Kneeling with her head bent, she bashed at the door till it fell off. Finally she set up the car jack between the seats, which were hanging from above. She and Ghotikar were as close as lovers. His salt-and-pepper hair was inches from her khaki-clad thigh.

"Is this your car?" she asked.

"A Chevy? Are you kidding? Haven't you ever heard the joke about how many bankers it takes to drive a BMW?"

"I don't like jokes," said Eureka, straight-faced.

So this was Serpas's car—or more precisely, the car he'd stolen from the woman in Atlanta.

"I was wondering why you're caught between the seats," she said. "Why not between the front seat and the dash? You must have been in the back seat when the car flipped over." Actually, given the force of the storm, anything could have happened. Still, it was a pretty good guess, and Ghotikar accepted it.

"I suppose you think I was in the back seat waiting for the guy," he said.

"Maybe you were crouched down with your gun, hoping to surprise him."

"Maybe I was assuming he'd come out to move his car to a safer place," said Ghotikar sarcastically. "That's what any responsible person would do when they heard a hurricane was coming.

But not Nat Serpas. You're not going to find him doing anything useful with his miserable life."

"I guess he's lucky he wasn't the responsible type," said Det. Kilburn. "Then you would have been able to shoot him."

"And what would be so wrong with that? You know he deserves it. And if you don't know, I haven't done my job. I haven't gotten across what a scumbag he is. He preys on women. Vulnerable older women."

It was true that in certain circumstances Eureka might step back and not interfere with frontier justice. There was no courthouse in Sarasota any more. No judges, either.

"You'd understand if you knew Bronwyn," said Ghotikar. "She was such a nice person. A real homebody. Of course she wasn't much of a cook. I had to do that, too, to get a decent meal. But she always tried her best. We did nothing to merit what happened to us. And I can certainly make whatever steps you take worth your while."

Det. Kilburn asked what he meant.

"I'm a very wealthy man. I don't want to brag, but I made more than ten men could spend in a lifetime when I was a banker, and now that I have Bronwyn's money, too, I can give you anything you want. How about a house in Iceland? It's so beautiful there. Cool breezes. Pure water."

Det. Kilburn wondered what she should do with someone who so clearly planned to shoot a fellow human being the next chance he got. Even if Serpas had killed his wife, she didn't see how in good conscience she could just release Ghotikar from between the seats. Not that that was going to happen in the next few minutes, anyway. She'd already tried three different positions for the jack, and none of them had worked.

"Serpas is in handcuffs," she said. "I saw him on 'CrimeWatch' just the way you did."

"Perfect. Forget me. Just go finish him off. I won't care if I never get out of this car. I can die in peace." He closed his eyes to illustrate.

"I know you're angry. But you don't really want to kill him. You'd be throwing your life away, and it wouldn't bring your wife back."

"I do want to kill him," he said, his eyes popping open down there next to the crushed roof. "I think of nothing else. I don't have a life any more, and it's his fault."

He was very convincing. She decided to confiscate his gun as soon as she found it. She wasn't even sure where she drew the line, but this was way over it, she was sure.

Besides, she wasn't sure he had the right man. What would Nat Serpas have been doing in Charlotte? Travel was very difficult these days. You had to have a powerful incentive to do it. You did not go from Atlanta to Charlotte and end up asking for work like some kind of hobo or yardman. Maybe if he'd met Bronwyn somewhere and figured she was a good prospect.... But Eureka couldn't see any way that would have happened.

The argument Ghotikar was supposed to have had with him made no sense. Serpas was not a day laborer, he was a con man. He was more likely to have tried to sell the Ghotikars pixie dust than to have mentioned any kind of violence. He might have gotten an advance to do contracting work that he didn't intend to do. That sounded like him. Or if he'd fallen on hard times, he might have offered to paint the hall so he could swipe some jewelry. But when he was turned away, why would he have threatened them?

As Det. Kilburn was thinking this through, she spotted Ghotikar's gun in the trunk. She reached out with her right foot and kicked it farther away.

"That's my property!" he said, immediately realizing what she was doing. "I'll give you everything I have for it!" He grabbed her arm with his upside down hand, but then thought better of it and withdrew.

Considering Ghotikar's role as avenging husband, it was odd the way he didn't dwell on murder or blood or even revenge. Eureka believed that if you paid close attention to the words people use, they inadvertently reveal themselves. Ghotikar was obsessed with work. When he spoke of Serpas, he talked about him the way you'd talk about an employee who didn't measure up. His bitterness seemed centered on a feeling of being deeply, thoroughly cheated.

Det. Kilburn knew then instinctively what job Nat Serpas had told Ghotikar he would perform and instead reneged on. She found herself asking, "Why did you get the lingerie for your colleague?"

"What lingerie? Where did you get that from? You knew all along who I was. I should have known." Ghotikar's sourness was returning. "I explained all that at the trial. I didn't buy any lingerie. Why would I? I wasn't interested in that woman. She wasn't my type at all. Anyone could have signed my name to the card. It wasn't even my handwriting. That's just the sort of prank the traders were always pulling. I can't be held responsible for what they do."

Nothing that happened at the bank would surprise Eureka. But she knew she was on the right track. Serpas had agreed to kill Ghotikar's wife. The two men must have first met in Atlanta. Businessmen like Ghotikar still traveled because of their professional responsibilities. Not everything could be done teleconferencing. He would have had meetings, consultations.

With advance in hand, Serpas should have been happy to sneak away—far away. But maybe murder was still too much for him. Maybe he drove to the Ghotikar house up in Charlotte intending to warn the poor woman. More likely, he wanted money from her in return for exposing her husband's plot against her.

So why was Ghotikar home at the time? Why wouldn't he have been as far away as possible with as many witnesses as possible? Because by then he'd seen Nat Serpas's photo on CrimeWatch and had learned he was a con man. He wanted to make sure Serpas was going to go through with his part of the deal. That time would have been only a test. He planned to ask him to come back later.

Eureka slipped out of reach of Ghotikar's arm as she pictured the scene on the porch up in Charlotte. A big old Victorian wrap-around, with plenty of room for everybody. Bronwyn would be puzzled at first by Serpas's accusations, more frightened of him than of her husband. But soon it would be clear to the banker that here was yet another job he was going to have to do himself.

Ghotikar was no fool. Far from his wrap-around porch, upside-down in a car that was no BMW, surrounded by trashed palm trees, he took stock of the situation and said, "You can't do anything about it. Double jeopardy applies."

"You tried to hire me to kill a witness," said Det. Kilburn, out in the sunshine once again. "That will cause problems if I manage to get you out of there."

✗

VALENTINE'S DAY

by John M. Floyd

Retired schoolteacher Fran Valentine pushed through the door of the sheriff's office with her purse clenched under one arm and a greasy paper bag under the other. "Want a donut?" she asked.

Sheriff Lucy Valentine hung up the phone and stared at her.

"You don't want a donut?" Fran said. "Are you sick?"

"What I am, is busy. Don't you ever knock, Mother?"

"Why should I? I'm a taxpayer—I own this office."

Lucy sighed. "I was about to call you anyway." She pointed to the telephone. "Penny Collins was kidnapped, three hours ago."

"You're joking."

"Am I laughing?" She squeezed her eyes shut and rubbed the top of her head as if trying to start a fire in her hair. "We found her car parked beside Lake Road. No witnesses. I just got back from her son's house—the state cops are already there."

"That's why you're sitting here doing nothing?"

"I'm not doing nothing," Lucy said. "And I'm sitting here because they sent me here. The staties are in charge now, and that means they want me and my deputies to stay out of their way."

"They used those exact words?"

"Let's see—they said, 'You and your deputies stay out of our way.'"

"Wait a minute. You said they were at the Collins's house? How'd they get there so fast?"

"Because they were here in town already, guarding the governor and the sheik."

Fran nodded and took a donut from her bag. "That's right, I forgot." The newly-elected governor was here for the day with the head of some Middle Eastern nation, touring the antebellum homes along the river. What a foreign dignitary was doing in a remote county seat in the Deep South no one seemed to know. Maybe he wanted to buy the courthouse. Fran added, "I came from home the back way, I guess that's why I didn't see them."

"Well, they're staked out at points all along the route. At least they were, until the Collins fiasco."

"And you weren't invited?"

"Maybe I misplaced my invitation," Lucy said.

She turned to her computer, verified that her latest Google search had found nothing useful, and keyed in another query. She didn't want to discuss with her mother, or with anybody, the fact that she and her office were often ignored by everyone in law enforcement above the county level. The lack of respect was even harder to bear because her late father had been the sheriff here for many years—but the reason for it was clear: Lucy Valentine was not only small-town, she was female.

The phone rang. Lucy answered it, a routine call from an elderly citizen to report a suspicious-looking stranger cruising one of the more affluent areas, and while she made a note and tried to reassure the caller she watched her mother from the corner of her eye. The truth was, Frances Valentine didn't much like the fact that her daughter was sheriff, even if it did mean Lucy was treading in her father's footsteps. Fran had informed her many times that not only was it a dangerous job, it was taking up too much of her time. It kept her from getting out and meeting other young people. Lucy knew all too well what her mother meant by "other young people"—it translated to "potential husbands." Fran wanted grandchildren, and the clock was ticking.

But the fact was, Lucy liked her work, and—although her superiors seldom recognized it—she was good at what she did.

She replaced the receiver and said, "Ludie Mae Russell. That woman's scared of her own shadow." She punched in numbers, reached Deputy Zack Wilson, and asked him to drive by Ludie Mae's house a few times, maybe even hit the siren once or twice. This actually killed two problems with one stone: she wanted to keep Zack away from the visiting bigwigs as much as possible—he was pushing eighty, and was more apt to shoot the governor by accident than keep others from shooting him. When she hung up this time she rubbed her head again with invisible shampoo and leaned back wearily in her desk chair.

"Aren't you supposed to use the radio to call your deputies?" Fran asked.

"The dispatcher's at lunch, and I'm tired. One of the blessings of cell phones in the field." Lucy had a sudden thought. "By the way—the attorney general's here as a part of the guv's entourage. He specifically told me he didn't want you meddling in this little issue."

"Cell phones versus radios?"

"The kidnapping case."

"Why would the AG say that?" Fran asked. "I don't even know him."

"He knows you. I guess he hasn't forgotten that you scared off that Federal agent last year."

"I kept him from arresting the wrong man. If you recall, he suspected credit-card fraud because he wouldn't believe a cherry bomb could destroy a mailbox full of—"

"You blew up a restroom in a public building, Mother."

"A trashcan in a restroom. A demonstration, for his benefit."

"A surprise demonstration. Anyhow, our esteemed AG said, 'You tell Frances Valentine to keep her nose out of this.' And those were his exact words."

Fran harrumphed and waved a dismissive donut, raining crumbs and powdered sugar all over the sheriff's desktop. "He's an idiot. Since when have I poked my nose into any of your cases?"

"Let me count the times."

"While you're at it, count the times I solved them." Fran seemed about continue, then paused, squinting. "Wait a second," she said. "Why would someone kidnap Penny Collins anyway? She's got no money—she's a retired teacher, like me."

"Come on, Mother. Her son's Martin Collins. Collins Enterprises?"

"But Martin and Penny aren't even on speaking terms."

"Maybe the kidnappers didn't know that."

"They're not very good kidnappers if they didn't." Fran sagged into a chair and took a bite of donut. "Ransom demands?"

"Two calls, so far. I was there for the second one."

"So you heard the suspect's voice?"

"And Penny's too. She was allowed to speak, I guess in order to convince her son she was alive."

"What'd she say?" Fran asked, chewing. It was the first time the sheriff could remember ever seeing her mother frown while eating something.

"She said she needed a doc."

"A doc? For what?"

"Who knows. She just said, 'Go back and find Dr. Thorpe.'" Lucy held out a hand. "Here, give me one of those."

Fran passed her the bag. "Was this message intended for her son?"

"I suppose."

"And that's all she said?"

"That's it. 'Go back and find Dr. Thorpe.'"

"I don't know a Dr. Thorpe," Fran said.

"Neither do I. Nobody does, including Martin." Lucy nodded toward her computer. "I've been checking—there's only one physician named Thorpe within two hundred miles, and he's a pediatrician in Memphis."

"And what about the 'go back?' What's that mean?"

"Beats me."

Lucy watched her mother mouthing the words several times, as if tasting them. Finally Fran said, "Maybe it's a clue."

"A clue to what?"

"Don't know. Maybe she's trying to tell us who snatched her, or where she is."

Both of them fell silent. Fran tilted her head back and studied the ceiling tiles. Sheriff Valentine finished her donut, licked her fingers, and took another. Outside the open window, the day was clear but as hot as hell's griddle. Birds sang in the oak branches.

"So where is she?" Lucy asked, her mouth full.

Fran kept her attention on the ceiling. "About what Penny said, on the phone…"

"Yeah?"

"Did you notice anything strange at all? Any pauses, any emphasis?"

The sheriff thought that over. "Actually, she hesitated for just a second, between the words 'find' and 'Dr.' And she seemed to drop the second 'd,' like 'find…Octor Thorpe.'" She dusted her hands together, adding more donut crumbs to those on her paperwork. "But that makes even less sense."

"Octor Thorpe." Fran stayed quiet a moment, as if weighing that. "And nothing else was said?"

"In the phone call? No. Well, yes, one thing, but it wasn't a message. It made me think they might be outside."

"Outside? What do you mean?"

"Penny slapped her face, or neck—at least it sounded like a slap—and said, 'Not gnats!'"

Fran turned to scowl at her. "'Gnats?' You sure?"

"Yep."

"But that's crazy—and whatever else she is, Penny Collins isn't crazy."

Lucy shrugged. "I'm just telling you what she said."

Fran sat up, then stared past the file cabinet and the fake potted plant and out the window in the direction of the library across the street. She looked, Lucy thought, like someone trying to spot enemy ships at sea through a heavy fog. A warm breeze through the window riffled the papers on the desk. Fran hadn't yet asked why the A/C wasn't on, so Lucy hadn't bothered to tell her it was broken again.

Fran said, out of the blue, "What are the stops on the governor's 'tour' today? Do you know?"

"Of course I know. Why?"

Her eyes came back into focus. "What are they?"

The sheriff pulled a printed sheet from the mess on her desktop and read aloud: "The Becker mansion, the Civil War memorial, the O'Reilly house, a speech at Stanton Park, and the Myers Plantation. Why, you want to join the parade?"

"I want to figure out what's going on," Fran said. "Something's funny about the timing, here."

"The timing of what?"

"You said Penny's words don't make sense. You're right, but I'll tell you something else that doesn't: a kidnapping on the day of the governor's visit. Anybody who'd snatch someone local, demand ransom, and plan ahead enough to make it all work, would also know the town'd be crawling with state police today. The Highway Patrol's probably thick as mosquitoes along that so-called tour route." She fixed Lucy with a stare. "Why kidnap somebody now, on this particular date?"

A good point, Lucy realized, but she couldn't see how the two could be connected. She just shrugged. Why do criminals do anything? If they were smart they wouldn't be criminals.

She ran a hand through her sweaty hair again and decided it was probably a good thing there wasn't a mirror in her office. Changing the subject, she said, "How well do you know Penny Collins?"

Fran bit into another donut and munched on it a while before answering. "We were never really close, I guess. We taught at the same school for years, so we saw each other every day, but we didn't get together after hours or anything. Your daddy was alive then, of course, so I wouldn't have wanted to." She frowned again, and her chewing stopped so suddenly Lucy wondered if her mother's peripheral functions needed to slow down, like dimming lights, when her brain was fully engaged. "But we both loved words and word games, I remember that. We liked puzzles, Penny even more than I."

"What kind of puzzles?"

"Any kind. Crosswords, Boggle, scrambled phrases, coded messages, anything—she was fascinated with them. Always worked the Jumble in the daily paper. We'd compete sometimes to see who could solve it first."

"And she won?"

Fran's frown eased up a little. "Not always." She finished her snack and wiped her hands with a napkin that looked as greasy as the bag it came out of. "Point is, we both liked word games, and—"

She paused, her napkin frozen in midair. Her face brightened.

"—and she would know that you'd call me to help on this." Fran stayed silent a moment, then nodded to herself. "She would know. So when she was allowed to say something on the phone to her son to prove she's alive, there's a good chance she'd say something with a hidden meaning, something that'd give me a hint about what's going on." She turned now to stare at her daughter. "Remember what I said earlier, about clues? There's something there, in what she said, Lucy—and we're missing it."

"I'm missing something in what you said. How would Penny know I'd call you?"

"Because you always do. You told me, when I first walked in here, that you were about to."

Lucy wasn't sure why that irked her, but it did. She shifted a little in her seat. "I was just going to tell you what happened. Not to ask you to get involved."

If Fran heard this lie, she gave no indication. Her eyes were narrowed to slits now, focused on something she could probably see only in her mind.

"The thing is, I need to handle this on my own, Mother," Lucy continued. "Dad taught me well—I know what I'm doing. Besides, I've been told to butt out of the Collins case. And so have you."

Still Fran didn't respond. Half a minute dragged by. Lucy turned back to the computer and Googled "Thorp, M.D." Without the E this time. Still no hits, at least none for locations anywhere nearby. What the hell had Penny been talking about?

Finally Fran said, "But that doesn't mean we can't work on it from the sidelines. Right?"

The sheriff looked up at her. "We?"

"What the attorney general doesn't know won't hurt him."

"You're saying you have some thoughts about all this?"

Fran sat up straight in her chair. "That call you heard. How much did the kidnappers ask for?"

"In ransom? Fifty thousand."

"To be delivered where, and when?"

"A place in the woods outside town, two p.m. today." Both of them looked at the clock. It was half past noon. "We've been ordered to stay away from there, too," Lucy added.

Fran seemed to ignore that. "But the state guys are checking it out, aren't they. Watching that area."

"I imagine so."

"More thinning of their numbers, and their attention," Fran murmured. "And fifty thousand's not enough."

"What?"

"I would have asked for ten times that, and gotten it."

"I don't follow you—"

"I think they asked for what they knew Martin Collins might have on hand, and could deliver quick." She fixed the sheriff with a stare. "Something's going on here, Lucy, I'm sure of it. Something beyond a simple kidnapping."

Lucy did a palms-up. "Even if that's true, what can I do about it?"

"You can hand me that notepad and pen," Fran said.

Five minutes later the sheriff's phone rang. She picked up, listened a minute, and blew out a breath. "Okay. You might as well get back on parade duty," she said into the receiver. She hadn't meant to use that term, but realized that what she'd almost said— "crowd-control duty"—would have sounded even more demeaning. She hung up and looked at her mother. "That was Malone." The other of her two deputies. "He's on his way back from the Collins's house."

"How'd he get to stay there," Fran asked, "when you didn't?"

"He had a civilian shirt in his car. I told him to put it on, and gave him my camera. Nobody looked at him twice."

"Impersonating a reporter. Good thinking."

Lucy shrugged. "It didn't help. He told me there are no new developments."

Fran, who had been doodling on Lucy's notepad and tapping one foot on the floor, stopped doing both and looked up at her daughter. "I wouldn't say that."

"There are new developments?"

Fran leaned forward, her face even more stern than before. "You said Penny's words were 'Go back and find...' etc. Right?"

"That's what she said."

"What if she meant 'go backward?'"

Lucy blinked. "Go backward how? Where? In time? Back to town?"

"Take the words 'Not gnats,'" she said. "You told me that was the last thing she said, on the phone. Remember what I said about her unscrambling words, working the Jumble? What if she meant, by 'go back,' that we should spell it backwards?"

"Not gnats?"

"Forget the exact spelling, and the silent G. Think of the sound—the way it sounds when it's said."

"What...?"

"Consider this," Fran said, waving her notebook. "What if I was right—what if the kidnapping is related to the visiting VIPs? What if whoever did this snatched Penny to complicate things, to create a diversion like we said? They might not care about the money. The two-o'clock drop time, and location, could be a complete lie. A misdirection." She lowered her voice. "What if these same people are planning something, for the event?"

Lucy's stomach went cold. "You mean like, a terrorist something?"

Fran hunched closer over the desk. Her eyes gleamed like a kid's on Christmas morning.

"What if," she said, "Penny heard them discussing their plans? What if she knew, at the time of the ransom call, what they were going to do? Or at least where they were going to do it."

"Spit it out, Mother. What have you found?"

Fran reached forward and slapped her notepad down in front of Lucy. On it, among the doodles, she had written the word NOTNATS.

It took the sheriff only an instant to spell it backward—and gasp. Silently Fran nodded toward the printed sheet on the desktop, the one with the list of tour stops.

Good God…

Heart thudding, Lucy snatched up the phone and punched numbers. Seconds later she said, "Malone? Head for Stanton Park. You understand me? Stanton Park. I'll meet you there."

"Why?" asked the voice on the phone. "What's happening?"

Lucy locked eyes with Fran and said to him, "You won't believe it."

The George J. Stanton Municipal Park, an open area with few trees and no surrounding buildings, was the least guarded of the stops the governor and his group were scheduled to make. After all, there were no visible risks—the place had clear sightlines and no good hiding places for a sniper or saboteur. As a result, only one man, Highway Patrolman Brian McAlpin, was posted there to monitor the scattered crowd, and he was tired and sweating and bored half to death.

He woke up a bit, though, when he saw a county-mountie roaring into the gravel parking lot, followed by another cruiser marked with a sheriff's star on its door. In the car with Sheriff Valentine was a woman the patrolman didn't recognize. The three of them piled out of the two cruisers and jogged in his direction.

"What's the problem?" McAlpin asked. Whatever it was, he wasn't worried. He'd been told to order the local lawmen away if required. Or maybe he should say lawpersons.

"We need to evacuate the park," the sheriff said. "Move everybody out."

He raised his chin. "On whose orders?"

"On mine." Sheriff Valentine turned to look east. "How long till the governor and his group get here?"

"Ten minutes. They're about to leave a place called the O'Malley house or O'Rourke house or some such, downtown. Why?"

"We've had a bomb threat, that's why."

That stopped him. "What?"

"You heard me. Divert the governor's party and help us get these people away from here." She glanced around and pointed. "At least past that corner."

Still the cop hesitated. This sheriff was a pretty lady—boy was she pretty, even with that rat's-nest hair—but he had his orders.

"I'm not sure I—"

"Now," the sheriff said.

Fran and Lucy helped Deputy Malone and the state trooper herd the crowd away and then stood and listened as the patrolman phoned his bosses and explained the situation. He didn't seem at all certain that he'd done the right thing, and from the look on his face the folks on the other end of the phoneline weren't pleased either.

Afterward, the sheriff and her deputy and the HP officer watched the deserted park in the distance, the crowd watched the cops, and Fran watched her watch. When fifteen minutes had passed, everyone's face—not just the patrolman's—showed doubt. Lucy's feelings went beyond that, to barely-controlled despair. The bomb-threat excuse had been Lucy's idea, a magic phrase that she'd known would get action. The truth was, they had no clue what might happen, here. If anything.

What if they'd misinterpreted Penny Collins's message? Lucy thought. Maybe the backward-spelled name was a coincidence. Or maybe Penny was crazy.

"Mother?" she said, her voice hushed. "What have we done?"

"Just wait," Fran said.

To the patrolman—Lucy didn't remember his name, so she checked the nameplate on his chest—Lucy said, "Was this area checked out this morning?"

"What for?"

"'What for?' For threats. Shooters, bombs, light sabers, anything. That's standard procedure, I thought."

McAlpin shrugged. "I hadn't been here long when you guys arrived. I heard each stop was being swept, but I doubt it got done. We've been spread pretty thin because of the Collins thing."

"The kidnapping?"

"A bunch of the force was out at the son's house earlier—you were there too, right? Now I imagine they're staking out approaches around the—"

"The woods north of town," Lucy said.

"Yeah, for the ransom drop." McAlpin was looking at her as if wondering whether she was really the sheriff or a loony impostor. "You mind telling me what this is all about?"

Instead of answering, Lucy sighed and stepped back to stand beside her mother.

"Be patient," Fran told her.

"Right," Lucy whispered. "I better patiently check for job opportunities for female peace offi—"

She never finished the sentence. The explosion, when it came, scared the bejesus out of her and everybody else. The decorated bandstand at the center of Stanton Park—the empty bandstand where the governor and his underlings and the visiting guest would have been standing at this moment if not for the change in plans—disappeared in a red fireball. Roiling black smoke darkened the sky, then was slowly pulled apart by the hot breeze.

It was so quiet they could hear the train whistle at the Murphysville crossing, six miles away. Flaming pieces of the wooden bandstand were raining down all over the park.

"What the hell...?" the patrolman blurted. His hat was off, his eyes bulging.

Lucy was staring too. When her pounding heart had slowed down a bit, she swallowed and said to him, "I think you better get the big boys in here."

"The big boys?"

"The Feds."

The next twenty minutes were—to say the least—hectic. At one point, though, Fran managed to pull Lucy away long enough to hiss something into her ear.

"What?" Lucy said. After what had just happened, she'd thought nothing could surprise her. "What did you just say?"

"I said we have to keep looking for Penny."

"But…" With an aching heart Lucy scanned the scene—the charred skeleton of the bandstand, the stunned spectators, the blackened earth at the center of the park. If whoever had done this also had Penny Collins, and had heard—or heard about—the blast…they wouldn't need a diversion any more. They'd just kill her. "Wouldn't we be too late?"

"We won't know unless we try," Fran said. "Right?"

Lucy raised her hands to rub her eyes, then let them drop. "You have any ideas?"

"A big one," Fran said. "About ten seconds ago." She held up her notepad. "Remember the old dog pound?"

"The what?"

"Not the Animal Shelter Center—I mean the old pound, on West Jefferson. It's empty now, but the sign's still on the front of the building."

"So?"

She looked Lucy straight in the eye. "I think that's where Penny is."

Minutes later Deputy Malone, his gun drawn for the first time in years, banged on the door of the abandoned building. When he received no answer, Lucy and Officer McAlpin forced their way inside from a back alley entrance. They found Penny Collins lying on the floor, tied and gagged but alive. A doctor was summoned to examine her. No one else was in the building.

Afterward, waiting on the sidewalk outside, Lucy said, "Well, Mother, when do you think I should get back into the stock market?"

Fran looked at her. "What?"

"To have solved this," Lucy said, "you must have psychic powers. Either that, or Penny does."

Fran chuckled. "There's only one thing Penny Collins and I have in common. But you're right, it did help tell me where she was."

"What's that?"

"We both taught English for thirty years."

"What do you mean?"

Before Fran could answer, the medics wheeled Penny out the front door of the building. As they passed, she held up a limp hand, and her escorts stopped the gurney.

Lucy and Fran stood there looking down at her. Penny, her face as pale as death, gave Fran a weak smile. "So, Frances. You figured it out. I knew you would."

Fran grinned. "In for a penny—"

"—in for a pound," Penny said.

The sheriff studied each of them for a moment before speaking. "What the hell are you two talking about? And Mother, how did you figure out where she was?"

"'Find Octor Thorpe,'" Fran said.

"Excuse me?"

Fran took her notebook from her purse, opened it, and on a blank page drew a "#" symbol, like the one on a telephone or computer keyboard. "That, Lucy dear, is an 'octathorp.' Also known as…"

Fran and Penny turned at the same time to look up at the age-faded lettering on the front of the building.

The sheriff followed their gaze. The words said DOG POUND.

"A pound sign," Lucy said.

Fran nodded. "The only one in town, far's I know."

Penny smiled again, and this time Lucy thought she saw some color in her cheeks. "Ah, Frances," Penny said. "Remember how the other teachers thought our puzzles were a waste of time?"

Fran wiggled her eyebrows and twirled an imaginary mustache. "The villagers told us we were mad."

The doctor appeared then and nodded to the medics, who loaded the patient and the gurney into the back of the ambulance. Lucy and Fran watched in silence as it pulled out into traffic.

After a moment Lucy said, "I still can't figure something, Mother. Why'd they leave her here? The kidnappers, or terrorists, or whoever. Why didn't they kill her?"

"They probably thought they were, by leaving her. The building's been empty for years—nobody'd think to search for her here."

Lucy nodded. Penny wasn't healthy to begin with, and as hot as it was today, in a boarded-up, unventilated building, without water…

She looked at her mother, squeezed her hand, and said, "You did good."

Fran shrugged. "We didn't catch the bad guys."

"We helped the good ones. You saved the life of a Mideastern leader—"

"Maybe."

"And a fellow teacher—"

"Maybe."

"And our governor—"

"I'm not sure if that's good or not."

"And there's a possibility Penny can ID the people who held her."

"I hope."

"So, overall," Lucy said, "I figure you had a good day."

Fran smiled. "You did too." She nodded in the direction of Officer McAlpin and the two deputies. "I told them you solved the case."

"You told them what?"

"And the message was passed upstream. I think your Rodney Dangerfield days are over."

"But, Mother—"

"Don't argue. This keeps me from having to talk to our idiot AG, and his fellow idiot the governor. And as for having a good day, well, my day isn't over yet."

"Why? You plan to save someone else?"

Fran checked her wristwatch and hitched her purse higher on her shoulder. "I plan to go to a bake sale. It's at Nancy Burton's, so it's not far. I'll walk."

Lucy looked around them in the street. It was clogged now with TV crews and reporters, and more were arriving every minute. "What about the media?"

"It's you they'll want to see. They wouldn't like the bake sale anyway."

Lucy couldn't help smiling.

"One more thing," Fran said. "That state trooper who helped us? McAlpin?" She pointed with her chin at the corner where he stood chatting with Deputy Malone. "He's kinda cute, don't you think?"

"I didn't notice, Mother."

"Well, I did. And he's not wearing a wedding ring."

Lucy sighed. "Why should that interest me in the least?"

"Because I invited him to your house for supper tonight, that's why. Seven sharp."

"You what?"

"I'll bring donuts," Fran said.

She was whistling as she left.

✗

THE BLACKHEATH COLLAPSE

by Sherlock Holmes

as Edited by Bruce Kilstein

As the official transcript of the trial has only just been published some twenty-two years after the events, I see it fitting to set down the facts of the case that have been previously unknown to the public.

April of 18__ found Watson and me under our annual attack on our rooms by Mrs Hudson and her band of spring cleaners. She chose a Saturday morning to launch her assault and, shortly after breakfast, ascended the stairs with an angry mop-and-broom-wielding horde and breached our dusty defenses.

"Right, Mr Holmes," she said, assuming a stance worthy of the Zealots, "we'll have you and the doctor out of 'ere promptly so that we can give your rooms a good going over."

Watson, startled, paused in mid-bite of toast and jam and gazed about our apartments as if for the first time noticing the accumulation of a season's worth of newspaper, pipe ash, clothing, correspondence, soot, and clutter. "She does have a point, Holmes," he admitted, self consciously brushing the crumbs into a neat pile on the table.

Finding ourselves outflanked and outnumbered, I folded the morning paper and, with a swift nod, our landlady unleashed her host of charwomen on the place. "Just as well. I suppose, Watson, that you wish me to accompany you to the rugby match."

He looked confused. "Why, yes, that would be most agreeable but, how on earth…?"

"Fret not over trivialities. You have eaten a more hearty breakfast than usual, suggesting that you may not have time for luncheon. You have done this in some haste, which means that you have an appointment, in those old shoes, which tells me that you plan treading on muddy soil. From your jacket pocket I note the brim of a small cap, no doubt in the colors of your team. I see in the paper that Blackheath is scheduled to play Blaydon at 2:00 PM. You could not have made your intention clearer if you had erected a banner. I accept your invitation."

The early fog had lifted and the day promised to remain bright. As the criminal classes of London had largely been in hibernation over the winter months, and no new cases of sufficient merit had presented themselves, I agreed to the day trip. I secured my cloak and stick and headed to the door. "You win, Mrs Hudson. Clean if you must, just don't touch anything." The maid had flung open a window and we were down the stairs to the street hailing a cab when the magnitude of her task hit her full force. Snippets of her tirade drifted down, "Look at this place…how am I supposed to… how can anybody…mercy sakes is that a live…"

I settled lethargically into the cab and Watson observed, "Fear not, my good man, some suitable havoc will surely soon be wreaked and require your services to set right. Meantime, a bit of fresh air and rugby will do you good." The cab dropped us at the station and we took the short rail trip south. The spring air filled the carriage as the greys of the city gave way to the lush green of countryside. I enjoy the vigour of exercise, and hold a particular fondness for those activities which may prove useful preparation for when the sticky moments of investigation call for close contact with ruffians—therefore, fencing or arts marshal such as Baritsu seem worthwhile endeavours to practice, whereas attending a game of golf or tennis as a spectator makes little sense to me. The attraction to the infernal sport of cricket, a favourite of Watson's friend Doyle, which seems presently en vogue to both play and watch, where virtually nothing seems to happen for days, eludes me. But Watson was correct in asserting that a day in the country would help break me from the feeling of ennui that accompanies times of mental inertia and, no doubt, divert the temptation to indulge in the seven percent solution of cocaine that I keep at my workbench for just such moments of boredom. Perhaps an afternoon amongst men locked in mock combat would prove bracing. We would soon learn that our presence at the match would provide the physical and mental stimulation that I had been craving.

Upon our arrival at Blackheath, Watson leapt from the cab and, judging from the spring in his step, shed the years and pounds that had accumulated in the intervening years since his days on the team. One cannot underestimate the quality and power of fond memory—the mere association with his old team—a conversation with old mates, or sharing stories and tips with the current players, seemed to invigourate the doctor more than any tonic or bromide that he could administer to a patient. Jolly good for him. The match had just begun as we took our places among the spectators behind the ropes on the Blackheath side. Watson waved to various acquaintances in the crowd and proudly donned his team cap.

The two sides were evenly matched with neither gaining advantage through most of the half. At one point they reached a stalemate and a scrummage was declared. The forwards of each team faced one another, arms locked around their teammates' shoulders. The foes then engaged and locked heads, like rams butting for spring mating rights, as the scrum half fed the ball into the tunnel formed between the lines. There ensued grunting, gnashing of teeth and a curious thudding that could only signify the knocking of opposing skulls. The crowds cheered for their respective teams, seeming to revel in this most dangerous part of a brutal game, like Romans cheering for their gladiators—as the ball came through, each side pushed the other with their upper bodies while using their legs to gain advantage of the ball. As so often happens, the tenuous balance of this human bridge was lost during the push/pull of diverse forces, and the scrum collapsed. The seething mass of arms and legs took several moments to untangle and, frightfully, when order was restored, one man remained face-down on the muddy ground. Cursory efforts to rouse the fallen player proved unsuccessful, and as the cry went out for a doctor, Watson bounded over the rope.

To my friend's credit, his heroic efforts to revive the downed combatant were admirable, however it was plain, even at some distance, given the utter flaccidity of the limbs and pallour of the features, that the player had expired. A hush fell over the observers of the sad scene and stretcher bearers were called to carry the body to the nearby clubhouse locker room. I accompanied Watson and the body, which was soon laid out on the massage table.

"What a horror, Holmes," Watson muttered as we bent over the deceased.

"What do you suppose happened, Doctor?" Jackson, the team trainer, asked.

"Crushed, in all likelihood," Watson said, mopping the sweat from his brow with a kerchief. "May have punctured a lung or else broken his neck in the scrum, whereupon breathing function ceased. Horrible, simply horrible."

"May I, Watson?" I asked, leaning over the corpse. A look of confusion came over my friend's face but he nodded assent. I performed my own examination of the neck and chest. "What is this man's name?"

"John, sir. Hubert John. Fine chap. So full of...life," Jackson fought back tears.

"There, there, buck up man." Watson attempted to comfort the trainer, placing a beefy arm across his shoulder.

I removed my notebook from my breast pocket and scribbled a quick message. "Come, Watson. Jackson has work to do, notifying the family and so forth. There is no need for a doctor at this moment." I led Watson away as the clouds of grief accumulated over what had begun as a promising spring day, and slipped the note casually to Jackson as we parted the gathering crowd.

I escorted my downtrodden friend back to the flat at Baker Street. In torpor, he flung himself into a chair by the fireplace. I rang for Mrs Hudson who arrived triumphantly to gloat over her handiwork in our afternoon's absence, but a quick glance at our strewn outer clothes and the mud tracked from the rugby pitch onto her freshly beaten carpet erased all pleasing notes from the joyful composition that had been her face. I raised my hand to silence the woman before she could begin her tirade. "Yes, yes, Mrs Hudson, I know. Doctor Watson has suffered a horrible shock. Please waste no time in bringing brandy!" The curtain of remorse that had fallen over Watson was enough to vouchsafe the gravity of the situation and she quickly left to fetch the decanter.

After some moments the restorative draught took effect and Watson found himself able to speak. "What horrid luck. Hubert was a pleasant chap. Not a bad forward either. One never knows what hand fate will deal you."

"True enough," I agreed. "But I think Mr John has been stricken down by the fist of premeditation rather than the random slap of fate."

Watson appeared confused, but before he could inquire into my line of reasoning, the bell rang and Mrs Hudson ushered in Inspector Lestrade.

"I came as quick as I could, Mr Holmes. What's all this about a murder?"

"Murder!" Watson leapt from his chair, spilling the remains of his glass on the already soiled carpet. I saw Mrs Hudson flinch but, bless her, she held her tongue and took Lestrade's coat and hat.

"Forgive Watson, Inspector, he knew the victim."

"Victim!" Watson shouted again, like some strange parrot in a Robert Louis Stevenson tale.

"I received your telegram, which was given by Jackson to the constable at Blackheath. If you are referring to the poor bloke who got himself crushed at the rugby match, then I am afraid that even you are mistaken, Mr Holmes. There must have been hundreds of witnesses, including Doctor Watson, who saw the man killed during play. While I admit that the incident was unfortunate, I hardly think…"

"Please, sit down gentlemen," I said. "I assume, in spite of your doubts, that you heeded my request and had the coroner sequester the body."

"Well," Lestrade admitted sheepishly, "Seeing as you have been a help to Scotland Yard from time to time, I did as you asked but I hope that we can put this matter quickly to rest as I am a busy man, you know."

"Quite. Well, seeing as we have some luxury of time before tomorrow's autopsy we can discuss the matter rationally."

Watson interrupted, "You were there, Holmes. It was plain that Hubert John was crushed at the bottom of the scrum. Death would have been unpleasant but, mercifully, it would have been quick."

"Surely the doctor would recognize a traumatic death," Lestrade added. "Spent enough time in Burma…"

"Afghanistan," Watson corrected, "The Northumberland Fusiliers…"

"…Afghanistan, to know what's what."

"Often we see but fail to observe," I cautioned. "Let us examine the facts. A pile of men fall upon one another in the midst of a rough and tumble sporting event. A man is found dead at the bottom of the heap and the first, natural, conclusion is that he was crushed by the combined weight of the throng. We had the unique opportunity to be on hand at the moment of demise and observe the corpus delicti. All the evidence is before us—we just need to be able to deduce from the facts the one true conclusion." My guests looked at one another, thinking I had taken leave of my senses, poor chaps. "In your experience, Watson, what are the mechanisms of death produced by a crushing injury?"

Watson stroked his mustache as he thought. "Well, if one is struck in the head, say by a hammer or club, the caving cranium may cause bleeding about the brain…but that doesn't seem to be the case here, there was no indication of skull fracture. An injury to the spinal cord in the neck will cause instant paralysis."

"Yet we know that this could not have happened," I interposed.

"Why not?" Lestrade and Watson answered simultaneously.

"In the excitement, you may be forgiven, or you may have forgotten, Watson, that you attempted to revive Hubert by means of assisted respiration and coronary massage—therefore, he was not instantly dead from a snapped neck, he was failing but not quite dead when you tended to him."

"You are correct, Holmes," Watson said. "I had completely forgotten. I suppose then, death came from crushing of the chest. A fractured rib could puncture the lung causing a dangerous bleed or pocket of air to collect around the heart, or," he added quickly, "he may have asphyxiated."

"If he had asphyxiated, he would have had an ashen or blue pallor, would he not?" Lestrade asked, pleased with his observation.

"Quite so. Bravo, inspector, your tenuous grasp of the obvious still holds. In the situation you describe, Watson, a filling of the chest cavity with blood or leaking air, what are the physical signs?"

"The side of the injury will be dull to percussion, the trachea will deviate away from the side of the injury, escaping air will enter the interstices of the soft tissues and the skin will swell, crackle, and crunch to palpation like a piece of toast."

A look of surprised realization came over my friend's face, which was sufficient for all present to indicate that none of these signs were present on the victim.

"Well, it would appear that we all have work to do," I said. "Monday, then, gentlemen, I suggest that we meet at the morgue and attend the autopsy. You will be so kind as to send word of the time of the inquest?"

Lestrade had removed a notebook from his breast pocket and was writing furiously "What?" he muttered, brow furrowed, looking up. "Oh, yes, certainly."

"I might further suggest that you obtain a list of all the members of both teams at the game today and make subtle inquiries as to why anyone would wish Hubert John dead."

Lestrade held up one finger in acknowledgement as he wrote. When finished, he turned abruptly and left, forgetting his coat.

The laboratory and morgue, which to the public may seem places of macabre machinations, are as a second home to the doctor and scientist who forge their many happy relations with both the living and the dead. Only from the study of the dead can much be gleaned about the living. In fact, Watson and I had first made acquaintance in the lab at St. Bart's during my study of the nature of the corpuscles of the blood. While the strict maintenance of a detached clinicism is necessary for our pathological investigation, it is perhaps much to ask when the subject for study on the slab is an acquaintance. And so I found the experience of witnessing the autopsy of Hubert John could cloud Watson's judgment (although he must have witnessed the death of comrades in Afghanistan—tasked with repairing what war had torn apart—I suspect that even a seasoned veteran would have little experience in the willful post mortem dissection of someone he knew). The work of the office of the coroner was, at best, erratic, and seeing as an extra medical opinion could do no harm, I took the liberty of wiring Watson's friend Dr Arthur Conan Doyle, and requested he meet our party at the morgue. The robust fellow was waiting for us when we arrived.

"Arthur," Watson said, obviously glad to see a familiar face in front of the house of death, "what an odd coincidence."

"No coincidence, John," Doyle said, embracing his friend warmly, "I'm here at the request of your friend, Mr. Holmes. Naturally, I read the sad news in yesterday's paper and came right away. Besides, I have been eager to meet the man about whom you have told me so much." Doyle extended his hand to me. "An honour to meet you, Mr. Holmes. John has permitted me to read some of the accounts of your cases. Quite stunning. I fancy myself something of a writer, but I have already contacted some publishers on Watson's behalf. There is some interest in publishing his stories; although, I have to admit some of the powers of observation he describes seem a bit..."

"Farfetched?" I ventured. "Yes, I fear that Watson has a gift for the dramatic. I've read a few drafts of his accounts of my cases—too much chasing of criminals and not enough of the process of detection." I checked my watch, noting that Lestrade, as usual, was late.

"In my studies at Edinburgh I had two professors, Doctors Bell and Cristinson, who made some astounding demonstrations using diagnostic forensics. Quite extraordinary," Doyle said.

I scanned the street unsuccessfully for signs of Lestrade. "Watson, Doctor Doyle was only at his surgery briefly today."

"He's quite right," Doyle admitted. "How...?"

"Quite elementary, Doctor," I said. "Once receiving my missive, you, no doubt, left in haste to join us. The whiskers on the side of your face are incompletely shaven and a bit of dry shaving soap has congealed in your ear. As I sent the telegram late in the morning, you, therefore, must have been doing something before your morning toilet, which would hardly include going to your medical practice ungroomed—morning exercise comes to mind; Watson mentioned you are fond of cricket but there would have been scant time for a match to conclude this early in the day—tennis, then seems more likely as bits of clay still cling to your stockings. After tennis, you felt a strain in your right shoulder, an awkward service or overhead shot I should think, and on the way home you stopped at your surgery to get some liniment as evidenced by the distinct odour of camphor and wintergreen, which I noticed when shaking your hand, accompanied by the unmistakable wince of pain in your shoulder when I shook it."

"Astounding!" Doyle said as Watson flushed with pride.

"Ah, Lestrade, nice of you to join us."

"Sorry, Mr Holmes," Lestrade said, out of breath, "Been rushing about all morning, taking down as many of the rugby players' statements as possible." He acknowledged the doctors and led us into the laboratory, signing in with the duty officer who granted us entry to the building. We proceeded down a narrow stairway to the basement morgue where the autopsy was already in progress.

Henderson, a good man, had already entered the chest cavity and as Watson approached, thoughtfully ordered his assistant to cover Hubert John's face with a cloth.

"Mr Holmes," Henderson said, "I am thankful for your interest in this case. Curious. Most curious." He held up one finger spotted in congealed blood and he reached into the chest cavity and conducted the removal of the heart. He turned the organ over in his hand for us to examine. "There is no significant evidence of enlargement to indicate a likely coronary." He placed the heart on a nearby bench and split it like an apple with a deft stroke of the scalpel. "The muscle tissue appears intact, the vessels show no abnormality." He shook his head.

"And I take it you found no blood or sign of a collapsed lung when you examined the chest," I stated.

"No, sir. You are quite correct. I admit, I was astounded to find the heart and lungs intact, as the description of the events of death were described as a crush injury during a rugby match."

"Curious. Damn curious," Doyle said. "Then, Dr Henderson, what is your diagnosis of the probable cause of death?"

"Did anyone know if the man was ill in the days prior to the event?" Henderson asked.

Lestrade spoke up. "I have interviewed his colleagues and teammates and all have informed me that he was in the most robust health."

"Then the most probable diagnosis would be a rupture of a brain aneurysm or embolus," Henderson concluded matter-of-factly, wiping his hands on his apron. "It will take some time to take apart the head of course, messy stuff for the funeral director to reassemble, but I am happy to do it."

"No need for that at the moment," I said. "But if it is acceptable to Inspector Lestrade, I ask you to refrain from signing a final report until we can clear up a matter or two."

"I have other work to do, I suppose I can take a break and come back to this later." He turned to Lestrade who shrugged and scratched his head. Henderson motioned for the body to be covered completely.

"Come, gentleman. Doctor Doyle, if you could come with us, I think your presence would prove invaluable to solve this little puzzle." Doyle agreed that he would be delighted to assist, and I led the party back to the street to meet Lestrade's waiting coach.

Lestrade said, "As there was no ring on the body I assume Mr John was unmarried."

"Sportsmen often remove their jewelry before competition," Doyle said.

"But the ring would still have left a mark on the finger, so we must still assume that he was a bachelor. Where should I direct the driver, Mr Holmes?" Lestrade asked.

"That would depend. We must answer the question of how Hubert died," I pondered aloud.

"Why aren't we considering a brain embolism as Dr Henderson suggested?" Lestrade asked, removing his infernal notebook and commenced his scribbling.

"What is the probability that the embolism should strike exactly at the beginning of the rugby match?" I asked Watson.

"Slim, bloody slim."

"Couldn't something have been, you know, jarred loose in his head during the play?" Lestrade asked.

"Can't say I've ever heard of that happening," said Doyle.

"Furthermore, in any suspicious death we must also ask: 'Who would have benefited from the murder?' Also: 'By what means was the act committed?'" I gazed through the small window of the coach. "If we eliminate the possibility of embolism for now, and there is no obvious sign of brain injury, nor is there evidence of lung collapse, then the only possible cause of death could be a sudden abnormality of the rhythm of the heart."

"A fibrillation or sudden cardiac arrest might not be detectible on gross examination at autopsy," Doyle agreed, his excitement rising.

"What agents could bring about such sudden collapse of circulation?" I asked.

"Toxins," Doyle said, "Perhaps the sting of a wasp or the bite of an arachnid."

Lestrade's head was pivoting rapidly back and forth between the speakers as the air grew heavy inside the crowded carriage. He was running out of pages in his notebook.

"Too early in the year for such creatures," I noted.

"And, no doubt, Henderson would have seen evidence of such at the site of envenomation. Poison, then. Hubert John was poisoned," Watson concluded, his grave statement halting Lestrade's persistent pencil. "If there are no external marks of poison, such as would be found with a dart or arrow as the savages of the tropics are known to do...."

"Then," Doyle interrupted, absently rubbing his sore shoulder, "the poison must have been ingested in some way!"

"Lestrade, have your driver take us to the Blackheath Clubhouse," I said.

We arrived at the quiet rugby grounds, which only two days ago had been a hive of excitement and sorrow, and made our way through the clubhouse to the locker room. We found Jackson, the attendant, about his duties organizing the place for the next practice session.

"Good to see you again, Dr Watson," Jackson said. "How may I help you?"

"Has anyone claimed Hubert John's personal affects?"

"I gave his wallet, watch, and clothing to the men from the coroner. All that remains are a few items in his locker. I haven't had the heart to clear them out yet—a spare jersey, hair brush, towel, and a few toilet articles." He gestured to John's locker.

"His family wouldn't want them?" Lestrade asked.

"Doubt it, Inspector," Jackson said. "Mr John was a bachelor." (Here Lestrade, pleased with having his deduction confirmed, eyed me with satisfaction as if he had solved the Ripper murders). "The only family I recall is a brother, an invalid, poor chap—polio, I think it was—and a sister who brought him to a match once. Very sad, really, one brother robust and running about the pitch, the other with no control over his arms or legs."

We approached the sad cubicle where the clothes hung with the limp pall of a flag at half mast. Lestrade removed a hairbrush from the shelf and reached for a small jar placed behind it. "I wouldn't touch that, Lestrade," I said. Lestrade withdrew his hand as if stung with an electric shock. "Dr Doyle, you have been invaluable in unlocking the key to this case," I said, removing a kerchief from my pocket and using it to remove the jar.

"Well, I'll be," Doyle said.

"Yes, it makes sense," Watson said.

"What does? Nothing makes sense!" Lestrade exclaimed, taking a few involuntary steps backward with Jackson peering over his shoulder.

"One method of poisoning is to ingest the compound, such as with strychnine or arsenic," Watson said.

"But the skin, Inspector," Doyle rushed in, unable to avoid finishing the doctor's conclusion, "is the largest organ of the body. And many toxins are readily absorbed through the dermis. A poison liniment would be a perfect vehicle!"

"Lord, have mercy," Jackson said. "Mr John did complain of a backache this week and he applied the liniment to his sore muscles before the game. I saw him do it."

"Poisoned ointment," Lestrade said, shaking his head.

"The next question we must ponder is: 'Who would have something to gain by Hubert's demise?'" I put before the committee. "In your inquiries, Lestrade, did Hubert have any enemies?"

"He was well-liked by his teammates."

"I'll vouch for that," Jackson said.

"I also inquired at his club and place of business," Lestrade said, flipping through his notebook. "No one seemed to harbour any ill will." Lestrade suddenly looked up, struck with a thought. "Maybe it was the brother! That's the ticket—he was jealous that he couldn't do the things Hubert could and wanted revenge."

"The final element to our questions, as you must know as an officer of the law, Lestrade, is to add motive, opportunity, and means of committing the crime. The killer must have had the opportunity to commit the act and I doubt his paralyzed brother would have been able to execute the heinous task. Jackson, do you by chance recall the name of Hubert's sister?" Jackson thought for a moment, "Yes, I do remember, a pleasant lady...Mrs Lamson."

"You have been most helpful, Jackson," I said. "Dr Doyle, if I am not mistaken, we are not far from your surgery. Might we impose upon you to make use of your rooms for our investigation?"

"By all means," Doyle said.

Conan Doyle opened his modest surgery where a second-hand desk and a fine layer of dust over his clinical bench suggested a medical practice that was far from busy. A servant, happy for some occupation of the vacant rooms, offered tea, to which Watson and Lestrade readily accepted, needing some restorative against the trying development of events.

"Do you have a London directory, Dr Doyle?" I asked.

"Yes, of course. Daphne, bring it at once, with the tea."

As the maid returned with the booklet and tea, I set out the jar of liniment on the desk. Removing the lid, I detected the peculiar odour I had scented on the body when it was removed to the locker room from the field. "Dr Doyle, do you possess tincture of atropine or belladonna?"

"Yes, of course. I have both." He removed two vials from a rack of chemicals.

"Excellent." I took a small spatula and extracted a small sample of liniment from the jar. "Watson, kindly pour Inspector Lestrade a cup of tea, won't you? Dr Doyle, if you would be so kind as to prepare a hypodermic of both the belladonna and atropine; I venture you may find them presently invaluable." Doyle raised an eyebrow and did as he was asked. "Inspector, kindly consult the directory and see if a Mrs Lamson resides in Cheltenham." Lestrade rested his cup on the bench and paged through the directory. While he was thus occupied, I removed a small cube of sugar from the dish, applied the spatula to it, and dropped the laced sweet into the policeman's tea. Watson and Doyle stood aghast.

"Here it is, Mr Holmes: a Dr George Henry and Mrs Kitty Lamson, 38 Malvern Road, Cheltenham, Gloucestershire."

"Lamson… Lamson," Doyle said. "The name is familiar."

Lestrade noted the address in his book and absently took a large gulp of his tea. After a few moments he said, "You don't think his sister…?" but, unable to continue the thought, became exceedingly flushed, sat his cup down and found his way stumbling to a chair. "Sorry, chaps, not feeling too well at the moment." He unbuttoned his collar. "The tea must have been too hot." He rubbed at his chest.

Watson rushed to his side and removed his watch. "Weak pulse, Holmes. I make it fifty, no, forty beats to the minute."

"Bitter taste to that tea," Lestrade said, as his eyes began to close. "What brand do you use, Doyle," he managed, as he lost consciousness.

"Holmes!" Watson yelled, as he frantically grasped for a stool and lifted Lestrade's legs. "You've poisoned him!"

"I have been wishing to do that for some time, Watson. Dr Doyle, if you would be so kind as to administer the atropine and belladonna."

With difficulty, Watson pulled the jacket off the lolling Lestrade and pulled up his sleeve. Doyle expertly plunged the needle into an exposed vein.

We watched and waited.

"Shallow respirations," Watson said, a strong note of concern in his voice.

"Slow, erratic heart rate. All signs of a bitter alkaloid," Doyle said.

"Aconite poisoning, I should think. Ah, look, our patient is responding to your tonic," I observed. Slowly Lestrade was regaining his senses. His crimson hue had faded to a safer shade of rose, and Watson nodded reassuringly to his watch as the heart grew stronger and more steady. "Could be a number of species of the plant—it grows all over the world—monkshood, Devil's helmet, leopards' bane—all members of the genus Aconitum."

"The liniment John rubbed on his skin would have worked its way into his circulation during the first half of the game," Watson said. "It's a good bet that Hubert would have been involved in some sort of pileup or collision by the time the poison took effect. Ingenious!"

"I should think a call upon the Lamsons would be in order. The Inspector should recover, but perhaps it's best we bring him along with a spare dose of the antidotes, as a precaution."

We assisted the dazed inspector back to the carriage and made our way to Cheltenham where we found Mrs Lamson at home in mourning for her brother.

"We are sad to intrude at this trying time," Watson said, making introductions. "I was an acquaintance of your brother at Blackheath."

"So kind of you to come to express your condolences, Doctor." She ushered us into the parlour of her modest home, eyeing the woozy Lestrade warily. "Your company is appreciated, gentlemen. I have not yet had the fortitude to notify my brother as yet. His health has been failing and, well, he's an invalid… and I was just off to the home to break the sad news."

"Yes, polio," Watson said, "We have heard."

"Poor Percy, his birthday is tomorrow. I was working up the strength to go to the sanatorium and bring him some small gifts."

"Madam, the news is grimmer than you know, I am sorry to say. Watson, some brandy from the small flask you carry," I said.

"I'm not thirsty just this moment," Watson said.

"Not for you, Doctor, for Mrs Lamson." I gestured to the confused woman as Watson withdrew the flask. "I regret to inform you that we suspect that your brother Hubert has been murdered." The news had the predicted effect and soon the doctors had abandoned the first patient and were attending the fainting woman. Lestrade fell onto a nearby settee, upsetting a jardinière on the way. We patiently waited for both to regain their senses. When the lady had been restored I asked, "May we inquire as to the whereabouts of your husband?"

She shook her head. "I regret to say that I have not seen him in several days. This is not unusual. He has been…unwell lately. Somewhat erratic in his behaviour, you might say." She began to weep. I nudged Watson to offer his kerchief. "I am afraid his use of morphine has become an addiction. We have fallen on hard times." She wept.

The sudden coalescence of the conclusion swept through my body as if I had injected myself with some drug. "You have my deepest sympathies. Might I ask what birthday your brother is celebrating?"

"Why, he will be twenty-one tomorrow."

"Quickly, men! We haven't a moment to lose!" The doctors dragged Lestrade to his feet as I escorted Mrs Lamson to our carriage and with all haste we sped the short distance to the sanatorium that was the residence of her brother Percy.

We were out of the vehicle before it had ceased to come to a complete halt and charged into the building. The attendant stood from his desk. "Why, Mrs Lamson, what a pleasant surprise. Master Percy will be joyed to see so many visitors on his birthday."

"Where is he?" I asked.

"In the solarium. Your husband, Doctor George, has just been here a few moments ago. He brought Percy his favourite—Dundee cakes, and the nurses have set up tea in celebration." He gestured toward the room at the end of a long hall.

"Hurry!" I shouted. "We may be too late!" We ran down the corridor, which ended in the bright room awash with the light from the many windows. At a small table a young man lay face down in a plate of cakes. Kitty screamed. Lestrade fainted.

"The antidote, Doyle!" I yelled.

We pulled the insensate Percy off the table and out of his chair. Watson tore open his shirt and Doyle plunged the atropine-loaded syringe between the ribs and into the poisoned heart. We waited hopefully for some moments, but it had soon become apparent that we had not arrived in time.

By then, the commotion had roused the hospital staff, who piled into the room. A curtain at the far end of the room rustled, and a man whose deranged look could only have meant he was Dr Lamson emerged and pushed his way through the crowd, dove through a window and tumbled onto the lawn in a shower of glass. Doyle and I were in immediate pursuit. Doyle ran well for a big man and we quickly overtook the fleeing fugitive, but he fought with the furious strength of one crazed on the wild effects of some mind-altering substance. Just as Lamson had broken free and was about to make it to the open field, he was struck blindside as if by a train. Watson, head low, shoulders square, took down the perpetrator with a textbook tackle.

When the mess was cleared, George Henry carted away, Percy's body taken to the morgue, Lestrade revived with another dose of atropine, and Mrs Lamson blessedly sedated, Doyle, Watson and I repaired to a nearby pub and partook of a long drink of bitters.

"I knew I recognized the name," Doyle said, wiping foam from his moustache. "George Henry Lamson studied at Edinburgh while I was there. He took a special interest in Cristinson's toxicology classes, but apparently never made it as a practicing physician."

"Chap grew desperate for money to support his evil drug habit. Even at the expense of his wife's family," Watson said.

"Bloody brilliant, tying up all the loose ends," Lestrade added, sipping tea and rubbing his head, "if I had not taken ill, I am sure I would have drawn the same conclusions."

"Yes, Lestrade, I am certain that you would have realized that aconite poison is drawn through the skin and it would take the skill of a deranged doctor to concoct such a lethal ointment to poison both brothers-in-law, making both deaths seem accidental, and all before the twenty-first birthday of Master Percy, so that the small inheritance he was due would fall to Mrs Lamson and so, by law, become the property of Dr Lamson, her husband."

"Fantastic, just fantastic," Doyle exclaimed, and raised his glass. "John, I have to apologize for ever doubting the skills of Mr Holmes or for thinking your accounts of his adventures mere fantasy."

"I couldn't have done it without your medical expertise, doctors," I said.

As an evening chill settled over London, Doyle and Watson made cheerful plans to publish a rousing account of the events of the case while Lestrade finished his notes and prepared to take credit for another sensational arrest. As the gaslights came up, I stared long into the darkness and wondered how I could have been so slow in my deductions to have not saved the life of Percy John[1].

---

1   Professor Cristinson had taught George Henry Lamson that aconite would be an undetectable poison, but by the time Lamson had graduated and carried out the murder, forensics had advanced to the point where this was no longer true, and his defense attorneys did not bother to call any scientific witnesses on his behalf. Lamson killed Percy with a laced Dundee cake for what would amount to only £1500 of inheritance money. In spite of public pleas made by his family and friends in America, Lamson was hanged for the crime in 1881. Strangely, the record of the trial was not published until 1914. This odd fact, combined with the significance that the first Holmes story Watson and Doyle published was 1888 (A Study in Scarlet) and that Holmes and not Watson only chose to record the events after the trial publication, makes one wonder if there is not some other important bit of mystery as yet unrevealed. It would be one hundred and thirty years until another aconite murder conviction in London: In February, 2011, a spurned Lakhvir Singh was convicted of killing her ex-lover by poisoning his leftover curry found in his fridge. A roommate had witnessed Singh remove the curry, and upon Singh's arrest, herbs containing aconite were found in her coat pocket.

THE FIVE ORANGE PIPS

by Sir Arthur Conan Doyle

When I glance over my notes and records of the Sherlock Holmes cases between the years '82 and '90, I am faced by so many which present strange and interesting features that it is no easy matter to know which to choose and which to leave. Some, however, have already gained publicity through the papers, and others have not offered a field for those peculiar qualities which my friend possessed in so high a degree, and which it is the object of these papers to illustrate. Some, too, have baffled his analytical skill, and would be, as narratives, beginnings without an ending, while others have been but partially cleared up, and have their explanations founded rather upon conjecture and surmise than on that absolute logical proof which was so dear to him. There is, however, one of these last which was so remarkable in its details and so startling in its results that I am tempted to give some account of it in spite of the fact that there are points in connection with it which never have been, and probably never will be, entirely cleared up.

The year '87 furnished us with a long series of cases of greater or less interest, of which I retain the records. Among my headings under this one twelve months I find an account of the adventure of the Paradol Chamber, of the Amateur Mendicant Society, who held a luxurious club in the lower vault of a furniture warehouse, of the facts connected with the loss of the British barque "Sophy Anderson", of the singular adventures of the Grice Patersons in the island of Uffa, and finally of the Camberwell poisoning case. In the latter, as may be remembered, Sherlock Holmes was able, by winding up the dead man's watch, to prove that it had been wound up two hours before, and that therefore the deceased had gone to bed within that time—a deduction which was of the greatest importance in clearing up the case. All these I may sketch out at some future date, but none of them present such singular features as the strange train of circumstances which I have now taken up my pen to describe.

It was in the latter days of September, and the equinoctial gales had set in with exceptional violence. All day the wind had screamed and the rain had beaten against the windows, so that even here in the heart of great, hand-made London we were forced to raise our minds for the instant from the routine of life and to recognise the presence of those great elemental forces which shriek at mankind through the bars of his civilisation, like untamed beasts in a cage. As evening drew in, the storm grew higher and louder, and the wind cried and sobbed like a child in the chimney. Sherlock Holmes sat moodily at one side of the fireplace cross-indexing his records of crime, while I at the other was deep in one of Clark Russell's fine sea-stories until the howl of the gale from without seemed to blend with the text, and the splash of the rain to lengthen out into the long swash of the sea waves. My wife was on a visit to her mother's, and for a few days I was a dweller once more in my old quarters at Baker Street.

"Why," said I, glancing up at my companion, "that was surely the bell. Who could come to-night? Some friend of yours, per-haps?"

"Except yourself I have none," he answered. "I do not encour-age visitors."

"A client, then?"

"If so, it is a serious case. Nothing less would bring a man out on such a day and at such an hour. But I take it that it is more likely to be some crony of the landlady's."

Sherlock Holmes was wrong in his conjecture, however, for there came a step in the passage and a tapping at the door. He stretched out his long arm to turn the lamp away from himself and towards the vacant chair upon which a newcomer must sit.

"Come in!" said he.

The man who entered was young, some two-and-twenty at the outside, well-groomed and trimly clad, with something of refine-ment and delicacy in his bearing. The streaming umbrella which he held in his hand, and his long shining waterproof told of the fierce weather through which he had come. He looked about him anxiously in the glare of the lamp, and I could see that his face was pale and his eyes heavy, like those of a man who is weighed down with some great anxiety.

"I owe you an apology," he said, raising his golden pince-nez to his eyes. "I trust that I am not intruding. I fear that I have brought some traces of the storm and rain into your snug chamber."

"Give me your coat and umbrella," said Holmes. "They may rest here on the hook and will be dry presently. You have come up from the south-west, I see."

"Yes, from Horsham."

"That clay and chalk mixture which I see upon your toe caps is quite distinctive."

"I have come for advice."

"That is easily got."

"And help."

"That is not always so easy."

"I have heard of you, Mr Holmes. I heard from Major Prendergast how you saved him in the Tankerville Club scandal."

"Ah, of course. He was wrongfully accused of cheating at cards."

"He said that you could solve anything."

"He said too much."

"That you are never beaten."

"I have been beaten four times—three times by men, and once by a woman."

"But what is that compared with the number of your successes?"

"It is true that I have been generally successful."

"Then you may be so with me."

"I beg that you will draw your chair up to the fire and favour me with some details as to your case."

"It is no ordinary one."

"None of those which come to me are. I am the last court of appeal."

"And yet I question, sir, whether, in all your experience, you have ever listened to a more mysterious and inexplicable chain of events than those which have happened in my own family."

"You fill me with interest," said Holmes. "Pray give us the essential facts from the commencement, and I can afterwards question you as to those details which seem to me to be most important."

The young man pulled his chair up and pushed his wet feet out towards the blaze.

"My name," said he, "is John Openshaw, but my own affairs have, as far as I can understand, little to do with this awful business. It is a hereditary matter; so in order to give you an idea of the facts, I must go back to the commencement of the affair.

"You must know that my grandfather had two sons—my uncle Elias and my father Joseph. My father had a small factory at Coventry, which he enlarged at the time of the invention of bicycling. He was a patentee of the Openshaw unbreakable tire, and his business met with such success that he was able to sell it and to retire upon a handsome competence.

"My uncle Elias emigrated to America when he was a young man and became a planter in Florida, where he was reported to have done very well. At the time of the war he fought in Jackson's army, and afterwards under Hood, where he rose to be a colonel. When Lee laid down his arms my uncle returned to his plantation, where he remained for three or four years. About 1869 or 1870 he came back to Europe and took a small estate in Sussex, near Horsham. He had made a very considerable fortune in the States, and his reason for leaving them was his aversion to the negroes, and his dislike of the Republican policy in extending the franchise to them. He was a singular man, fierce and quick-tempered, very foul-mouthed when he was angry, and of a most retiring disposition. During all the years that he lived at Horsham, I doubt if ever he set foot in the town. He had a garden and two or three fields round his house, and there he would take his exercise, though very often for weeks on end he would never leave his room. He drank a great deal of brandy and smoked very heavily, but he would see no society and did not want any friends, not even his own brother.

"He didn't mind me; in fact, he took a fancy to me, for at the time when he saw me first I was a youngster of twelve or so. This would be in the year 1878, after he had been eight or nine years in England. He begged my father to let me live with him and he was very kind to me in his way. When he was sober he used to be fond of playing backgammon and draughts with me, and he would make me his representative both with the servants and with the tradespeople, so that by the time that I was sixteen I was quite master of the house. I kept all the keys and could go where I liked and do what I liked, so long as I did not disturb him in his privacy. There was one singular exception, however, for he had a single room, a lumber-room up among the attics, which was invariably locked, and which he would never permit either me or anyone else to enter. With a boy's curiosity I have peeped through the keyhole, but I was never able to see more than such a collection of old trunks and bundles as would be expected in such a room.

"One day—it was in March, 1883—a letter with a foreign stamp lay upon the table in front of the colonel's plate. It was not a common thing for him to receive letters, for his bills were all paid in ready money, and he had no friends of any sort. 'From India!' said he as he took it up, 'Pondicherry postmark! What can this be?' Opening it hurriedly, out there jumped five little dried orange pips, which pattered down upon his plate. I began to laugh at this, but the laugh was struck from my lips at the sight of his face. His lip had fallen, his eyes were protruding, his skin the colour of putty, and he glared at the envelope which he still held in his trembling hand, 'K. K. K.!' he shrieked, and then, 'My God, my God, my sins have overtaken me!'

"'What is it, uncle?' I cried.

"'Death,' said he, and rising from the table he retired to his room, leaving me palpitating with horror. I took up the envelope and saw scrawled in red ink upon the inner flap, just above the gum, the letter K three times repeated. There was nothing else save the five dried pips. What could be the reason of his overpowering terror? I left the breakfast-table, and as I ascended the stair I met him coming down with an old rusty key, which must have belonged to the attic, in one hand, and a small brass box, like a cashbox, in the other.

"'They may do what they like, but I'll checkmate them still,' said he with an oath. 'Tell Mary that I shall want a fire in my room to-day, and send down to Fordham, the Horsham lawyer.'

"I did as he ordered, and when the lawyer arrived I was asked to step up to the room. The fire was burning brightly, and in the grate there was a mass of black, fluffy ashes, as of burned paper, while the brass box stood open and empty beside it. As I glanced at the box I noticed, with a start, that upon the lid was printed the treble K which I had read in the morning upon the envelope.

"'I wish you, John,' said my uncle, 'to witness my will. I leave my estate, with all its advantages and all its disadvantages, to my brother, your father, whence it will, no doubt, descend to you. If you can enjoy it in peace, well and good! If you find you cannot, take my advice, my boy, and leave it to your deadliest enemy. I am sorry to give you such a two-edged thing, but I can't say what turn things are going to take. Kindly sign the paper where Mr Fordham shows you.'

"I signed the paper as directed, and the lawyer took it away with him. The singular incident made, as you may think, the deepest impression upon me, and I pondered over it and turned it every way in my mind without being able to make anything of it. Yet I could not shake off the vague feeling of dread which it left behind, though the sensation grew less keen as the weeks passed and nothing happened to disturb the usual routine of our lives. I could see a change in my uncle, however. He drank more than ever, and he was less inclined for any sort of society. Most of his time he would spend in his room, with the door locked upon the inside, but sometimes he would emerge in a sort of drunken frenzy and would burst out of the house and tear about the garden with a revolver in his hand, screaming out that he was afraid of no man, and that he was not to be cooped up, like a sheep in a pen, by man or devil. When these hot fits were over, however, he would rush tumultuously in at the door and lock and bar it behind him, like a man who can brazen it out no longer against the terror which lies at the roots of his soul. At such times I have seen his face, even on a cold day, glisten with moisture, as though it were new raised from a basin.

"Well, to come to an end of the matter, Mr Holmes, and not to abuse your patience, there came a night when he made one of those drunken sallies from which he never came back. We found him, when we went to search for him, face downward in a little green-scummed pool, which lay at the foot of the garden. There was no sign of any violence, and the water was but two feet deep, so that the jury, having regard to his known eccentricity, brought in a verdict of 'suicide.' But I, who knew how he winced from the very thought of death, had much ado to persuade myself that he had gone out of his way to meet it. The matter passed, however, and my father entered into possession of the estate, and of some 14,000 pounds, which lay to his credit at the bank."

"One moment," Holmes interposed, "your statement is, I foresee, one of the most remarkable to which I have ever listened. Let me have the date of the reception by your uncle of the letter, and the date of his supposed suicide."

"The letter arrived on March 10, 1883. His death was seven weeks later, upon the night of May 2nd."

"Thank you. Pray proceed."

"When my father took over the Horsham property, he, at my request, made a careful examination of the attic, which had been always locked up. We found the brass box there, although its contents had been destroyed. On the inside of the cover was a paper label, with the initials of K. K. K. repeated upon it, and 'Letters, memoranda, receipts, and a register' written beneath. These, we presume, indicated the nature of the papers which had been destroyed by Colonel Openshaw. For the rest, there was nothing of much importance in the attic save a great many scattered papers and note-books bearing upon my uncle's life in America. Some of them were of the war time and showed that he had done his duty well and had borne the repute of a brave soldier. Others were of a date during the reconstruction of the Southern states, and were mostly concerned with politics, for he had evidently taken a strong part in opposing the carpet-bag politicians who had been sent down from the North.

"Well, it was the beginning of '84 when my father came to live at Horsham, and all went as well as possible with us until the January of '85. On the fourth day after the new year I heard my father give a sharp cry of surprise as we sat together at the breakfast-table. There he was, sitting with a newly opened envelope in one hand and five dried orange pips in the outstretched palm of the other one. He had always laughed at what he called my cock-and-bull story about the colonel, but he looked very scared and puzzled now that the same thing had come upon himself.

"'Why, what on earth does this mean, John?' he stammered.

"My heart had turned to lead. 'It is K. K. K.,' said I.

"He looked inside the envelope. 'So it is,' he cried. 'Here are the very letters. But what is this written above them?'

"'Put the papers on the sundial,' I read, peeping over his shoulder.

"'What papers? What sundial?' he asked.

"'The sundial in the garden. There is no other,' said I; 'but the papers must be those that are destroyed.'

"'Pooh!' said he, gripping hard at his courage. 'We are in a civilised land here, and we can't have tomfoolery of this kind. Where does the thing come from?'

"'From Dundee,' I answered, glancing at the postmark.

"'Some preposterous practical joke,' said he. 'What have I to do with sundials and papers? I shall take no notice of such nonsense.'

"'I should certainly speak to the police,' I said.

"'And be laughed at for my pains. Nothing of the sort.'

"'Then let me do so?'

"'No, I forbid you. I won't have a fuss made about such nonsense.'

"It was in vain to argue with him, for he was a very obstinate man. I went about, however, with a heart which was full of forebodings.

"On the third day after the coming of the letter my father went from home to visit an old friend of his, Major Freebody, who is in command of one of the forts upon Portsdown Hill. I was glad that he should go, for it seemed to me that he was farther from danger when he was away from home. In that, however, I was in error. Upon the second day of his absence I received a telegram from the major, imploring me to come at once. My father had fallen over one of the deep chalk-pits which abound in the neighbourhood, and was lying senseless, with a shattered skull. I hurried to him, but he passed away without having ever recovered his consciousness. He had, as it appears, been returning from Fareham in the twilight, and as the country was unknown to him, and the chalk-pit unfenced, the jury had no hesitation in bringing in a verdict of 'death from accidental causes.' Carefully as I examined every fact connected with his death, I was unable to find anything which could suggest the idea of murder. There were no signs of violence, no footmarks, no robbery, no record of strangers having been seen upon the roads. And yet I need not tell you that my mind was far from at ease, and that I was well-nigh certain that some foul plot had been woven round him.

"In this sinister way I came into my inheritance. You will ask me why I did not dispose of it? I answer, because I was well convinced that our troubles were in some way dependent upon an incident in my uncle's life, and that the danger would be as pressing in one house as in another.

"It was in January, '85, that my poor father met his end, and two years and eight months have elapsed since then. During that time I have lived happily at Horsham, and I had begun to hope that this curse had passed away from the family, and that it had ended with the last generation. I had begun to take comfort too soon, however; yesterday morning the blow fell in the very shape in which it had come upon my father."

The young man took from his waistcoat a crumpled envelope, and turning to the table he shook out upon it five little dried orange pips.

"This is the envelope," he continued. "The postmark is London—eastern division. Within are the very words which were upon my father's last message: 'K. K. K.'; and then 'Put the papers on the sundial.'"

"What have you done?" asked Holmes.

"Nothing."

"Nothing?"

"To tell the truth"—he sank his face into his thin, white hands—"I have felt helpless. I have felt like one of those poor rabbits when the snake is writhing towards it. I seem to be in the grasp of some resistless, inexorable evil, which no foresight and no precautions can guard against."

"Tut! tut!" cried Sherlock Holmes. "You must act, man, or you are lost. Nothing but energy can save you. This is no time for despair."

"I have seen the police."

"Ah!"

"But they listened to my story with a smile. I am convinced that the inspector has formed the opinion that the letters are all practical jokes, and that the deaths of my relations were really accidents, as the jury stated, and were not to be connected with the warnings."

Holmes shook his clenched hands in the air. "Incredible imbecility!" he cried.

"They have, however, allowed me a policeman, who may remain in the house with me."

"Has he come with you to-night?"

"No. His orders were to stay in the house."

Again Holmes raved in the air.

"Why did you come to me," he cried, "and, above all, why did you not come at once?"

"I did not know. It was only to-day that I spoke to Major Prendergast about my troubles and was advised by him to come to you."

"It is really two days since you had the letter. We should have acted before this. You have no further evidence, I suppose, than that which you have placed before us—no suggestive detail which might help us?"

"There is one thing," said John Openshaw. He rummaged in his coat pocket, and, drawing out a piece of discoloured, blue-tinted paper, he laid it out upon the table. "I have some remembrance," said he, "that on the day when my uncle burned the papers I observed that the small, unburned margins which lay amid the ashes were of this particular colour. I found this single sheet upon the floor of his room, and I am inclined to think that it may be one of the papers which has, perhaps, fluttered out from among the others, and in that way has escaped destruction. Beyond the mention of pips, I do not see that it helps us much. I think myself that it is a page from some private diary. The writing is undoubtedly my uncle's."

Holmes moved the lamp, and we both bent over the sheet of paper, which showed by its ragged edge that it had indeed been torn from a book. It was headed, "March, 1869," and beneath were the following enigmatical notices:

"4th. Hudson came. Same old platform.

"7th. Set the pips on McCauley, Paramore, and John Swain, of St. Augustine.

"9th. McCauley cleared.

"10th. John Swain cleared.

"12th. Visited Paramore. All well."

"Thank you!" said Holmes, folding up the paper and returning it to our visitor. "And now you must on no account lose another instant. We cannot spare time even to discuss what you have told me. You must get home instantly and act."

"What shall I do?"

"There is but one thing to do. It must be done at once. You must put this piece of paper which you have shown us into the brass box which you have described. You must also put in a note to say that all the other papers were burned by your uncle, and that this is the only one which remains. You must assert that in such words as will carry conviction with them. Having done this, you must at once put the box out upon the sundial, as directed. Do you understand?"

"Entirely."

"Do not think of revenge, or anything of the sort, at present. I think that we may gain that by means of the law; but we have our web to weave, while theirs is already woven. The first consideration is to remove the pressing danger which threatens you. The second is to clear up the mystery and to punish the guilty parties."

"I thank you," said the young man, rising and pulling on his overcoat. "You have given me fresh life and hope. I shall certainly do as you advise."

"Do not lose an instant. And, above all, take care of yourself in the meanwhile, for I do not think that there can be a doubt that you are threatened by a very real and imminent danger. How do you go back?"

"By train from Waterloo."

"It is not yet nine. The streets will be crowded, so I trust that you may be in safety. And yet you cannot guard yourself too closely."

"I am armed."

"That is well. To-morrow I shall set to work upon your case."

"I shall see you at Horsham, then?"

"No, your secret lies in London. It is there that I shall seek it."

"Then I shall call upon you in a day, or in two days, with news as to the box and the papers. I shall take your advice in every particular." He shook hands with us and took his leave. Outside the wind still screamed and the rain splashed and pattered against the windows. This strange, wild story seemed to have come to us from amid the mad elements—blown in upon us like a sheet of sea-weed in a gale—and now to have been reabsorbed by them once more.

Sherlock Holmes sat for some time in silence, with his head sunk forward and his eyes bent upon the red glow of the fire. Then he lit his pipe, and leaning back in his chair he watched the blue smoke-rings as they chased each other up to the ceiling.

"I think, Watson," he remarked at last, "that of all our cases we have had none more fantastic than this."

"Save, perhaps, the Sign of Four."

"Well, yes. Save, perhaps, that. And yet this John Openshaw seems to me to be walking amid even greater perils than did the Sholtos."

"But have you," I asked, "formed any definite conception as to what these perils are?"

"There can be no question as to their nature," he answered.

"Then what are they? Who is this K. K. K., and why does he pursue this unhappy family?"

Sherlock Holmes closed his eyes and placed his elbows upon the arms of his chair, with his finger-tips together. "The ideal reasoner," he remarked, "would, when he had once been shown a single fact in all its bearings, deduce from it not only all the chain of events which led up to it but also all the results which would follow from it. As Cuvier could correctly describe a whole animal by the contemplation of a single bone, so the observer who has thoroughly understood one link in a series of incidents should be able to accurately state all the other ones, both before and after. We have not yet grasped the results which the reason alone can attain to. Problems may be solved in the study which have baffled all those who have sought a solution by the aid of their senses. To carry the art, however, to its highest pitch, it is necessary that the reasoner should be able to utilise all the facts which have come to his knowledge; and this in itself implies, as you will readily see, a possession of all knowledge, which, even in these days of free education and encyclopaedias, is a somewhat rare accomplishment. It is not so impossible, however, that a man should possess all knowledge which is likely to be useful to him in his work, and this I have endeavoured in my case to do. If I remember rightly, you on one occasion, in the early days of our friendship, defined my limits in a very precise fashion."

"Yes," I answered, laughing. "It was a singular document. Philosophy, astronomy, and politics were marked at zero, I remember. Botany variable, geology profound as regards the mud-stains from any region within fifty miles of town, chemistry eccentric, anatomy unsystematic, sensational literature and crime records unique, violin-player, boxer, swordsman, lawyer, and self-poisoner by cocaine and tobacco. Those, I think, were the main points of my analysis."

Holmes grinned at the last item. "Well," he said, "I say now, as I said then, that a man should keep his little brain-attic stocked with all the furniture that he is likely to use, and the rest he can put away in the lumber-room of his library, where he can get it if he wants it. Now, for such a case as the one which has been submitted to us to-night, we need certainly to muster all our resources. Kindly hand me down the letter K of the 'American Encyclopaedia' which stands upon the shelf beside you. Thank you. Now let us consider the situation and see what may be deduced from it. In the first place, we may start with a strong presumption that Colonel Openshaw had some very strong reason for leaving America. Men at his time of life do not change all their habits and exchange willingly the charming climate of Florida for the lonely life of an English provincial town. His extreme love of solitude in England suggests the idea that he was in fear of someone or something, so we may assume as a working hypothesis that it was fear of someone or something which drove him from America. As to what it was he feared, we can only deduce that by considering the formidable letters which were received by himself and his successors. Did you remark the postmarks of those letters?"

"The first was from Pondicherry, the second from Dundee, and the third from London."

"From East London. What do you deduce from that?"

"They are all seaports. That the writer was on board of a ship."

"Excellent. We have already a clue. There can be no doubt that the probability—the strong probability—is that the writer was on board of a ship. And now let us consider another point. In the case of Pondicherry, seven weeks elapsed between the threat and its fulfilment, in Dundee it was only some three or four days. Does that suggest anything?"

"A greater distance to travel."

"But the letter had also a greater distance to come."

"Then I do not see the point."

"There is at least a presumption that the vessel in which the man or men are is a sailing-ship. It looks as if they always send their singular warning or token before them when starting upon their mission. You see how quickly the deed followed the sign when it came from Dundee. If they had come from Pondicherry in a steamer they would have arrived almost as soon as their letter. But, as a matter of fact, seven weeks elapsed. I think that those seven weeks represented the difference between the mail-boat which brought the letter and the sailing vessel which brought the writer."

"It is possible."

"More than that. It is probable. And now you see the deadly urgency of this new case, and why I urged young Openshaw to caution. The blow has always fallen at the end of the time which it would take the senders to travel the distance. But this one comes from London, and therefore we cannot count upon delay."

"Good God!" I cried. "What can it mean, this relentless persecution?"

"The papers which Openshaw carried are obviously of vital importance to the person or persons in the sailing-ship. I think that it is quite clear that there must be more than one of them. A single man could not have carried out two deaths in such a way as to deceive a coroner's jury. There must have been several in it, and they must have been men of resource and determination. Their papers they mean to have, be the holder of them who it may. In this way you see K. K. K. ceases to be the initials of an individual and becomes the badge of a society."

"But of what society?"

"Have you never—" said Sherlock Holmes, bending forward and sinking his voice—"have you never heard of the Ku Klux Klan?"

"I never have."

Holmes turned over the leaves of the book upon his knee. "Here it is," said he presently:

"'Ku Klux Klan. A name derived from the fanciful resemblance to the sound produced by cocking a rifle. This terrible secret society was formed by some ex-Confederate soldiers in the Southern states after the Civil War, and it rapidly formed local branches in different parts of the country, notably in Tennessee, Louisiana, the Carolinas, Georgia, and Florida. Its power was used for political purposes, principally for the terrorising of the negro voters and the murdering and driving from the country of those who were opposed to its views. Its outrages were usually preceded by a warning sent to the marked man in some fantastic but generally recognised shape—a sprig of oak-leaves in some parts, melon seeds or orange pips in others. On receiving this the victim might either openly abjure his former ways, or might fly from the country. If he braved the matter out, death would unfailingly come upon him, and usually in some strange and unforeseen manner. So perfect was the organisation of the society, and so systematic its methods, that there is hardly a case upon record where any man succeeded in braving it with impunity, or in which any of its outrages were traced home to the perpetrators. For some years the organisation flourished in spite of the efforts of the United States government and of the better classes of the community in the South. Eventually, in the year 1869, the movement rather suddenly collapsed, although there have been sporadic outbreaks of the same sort since that date.'

"You will observe," said Holmes, laying down the volume, "that the sudden breaking up of the society was coincident with the disappearance of Openshaw from America with their papers. It may well have been cause and effect. It is no wonder that he and his family have some of the more implacable spirits upon their track. You can understand that this register and diary may implicate some of the first men in the South, and that there may be many who will not sleep easy at night until it is recovered."

"Then the page we have seen—"

"Is such as we might expect. It ran, if I remember right, 'sent the pips to A, B, and C'—that is, sent the society's warning to them. Then there are successive entries that A and B cleared, or left the country, and finally that C was visited, with, I fear, a sinister result for C. Well, I think, Doctor, that we may let some light into this dark place, and I believe that the only chance young Openshaw has in the meantime is to do what I have told him. There is nothing more to be said or to be done to-night, so hand me over my violin and let us try to forget for half an hour the miserable weather and the still more miserable ways of our fellow-men."

It had cleared in the morning, and the sun was shining with a subdued brightness through the dim veil which hangs over the great city. Sherlock Holmes was already at breakfast when I came down.

"You will excuse me for not waiting for you," said he; "I have, I foresee, a very busy day before me in looking into this case of young Openshaw's."

"What steps will you take?" I asked.

"It will very much depend upon the results of my first inquiries. I may have to go down to Horsham, after all."

"You will not go there first?"

"No, I shall commence with the City. Just ring the bell and the maid will bring up your coffee."

As I waited, I lifted the unopened newspaper from the table and glanced my eye over it. It rested upon a heading which sent a chill to my heart.

"Holmes," I cried, "you are too late."

"Ah!" said he, laying down his cup, "I feared as much. How was it done?" He spoke calmly, but I could see that he was deeply moved.

"My eye caught the name of Openshaw, and the heading 'Tragedy Near Waterloo Bridge.' Here is the account:

"Between nine and ten last night Police-Constable Cook, of the H Division, on duty near Waterloo Bridge, heard a cry for help and a splash in the water. The night, however, was extremely dark and stormy, so that, in spite of the help of several passers-by, it was quite impossible to effect a rescue. The alarm, however, was given, and, by the aid of the water-police, the body was eventually recovered. It proved to be that of a young gentleman whose name, as it appears from an envelope which was found in his pocket, was John Openshaw, and whose residence is near Horsham. It is conjectured that he may have been hurrying down to catch the last train from Waterloo Station, and that in his haste and the extreme darkness he missed his path and walked over the edge of one of the small landing-places for river steamboats. The body exhibited no traces of violence, and there can be no doubt that the deceased had been the victim of an unfortunate accident, which should have the effect of calling the attention of the authorities to the condition of the riverside landing-stages."

We sat in silence for some minutes, Holmes more depressed and shaken than I had ever seen him.

"That hurts my pride, Watson," he said at last. "It is a petty feeling, no doubt, but it hurts my pride. It becomes a personal matter with me now, and, if God sends me health, I shall set my hand upon this gang. That he should come to me for help, and that I should send him away to his death—!" He sprang from his chair and paced about the room in uncontrollable agitation, with a flush upon his sallow cheeks and a nervous clasping and unclasping of his long thin hands.

"They must be cunning devils," he exclaimed at last. "How could they have decoyed him down there? The Embankment is not on the direct line to the station. The bridge, no doubt, was too crowded, even on such a night, for their purpose. Well, Watson, we shall see who will win in the long run. I am going out now!"

"To the police?"

"No; I shall be my own police. When I have spun the web they may take the flies, but not before."

All day I was engaged in my professional work, and it was late in the evening before I returned to Baker Street. Sherlock Holmes had not come back yet. It was nearly ten o'clock before he entered, looking pale and worn. He walked up to the sideboard, and tearing a piece from the loaf he devoured it voraciously, washing it down with a long draught of water.

"You are hungry," I remarked.

"Starving. It had escaped my memory. I have had nothing since breakfast."

"Nothing?"

"Not a bite. I had no time to think of it."

"And how have you succeeded?"

"Well."

"You have a clue?"

"I have them in the hollow of my hand. Young Openshaw shall not long remain unavenged. Why, Watson, let us put their own devilish trade-mark upon them. It is well thought of!"

"What do you mean?"

He took an orange from the cupboard, and tearing it to pieces he squeezed out the pips upon the table. Of these he took five and thrust them into an envelope. On the inside of the flap he wrote "S. H. for J. O." Then he sealed it and addressed it to "Captain James Calhoun, Barque 'Lone Star,' Savannah, Georgia."

"That will await him when he enters port," said he, chuckling. "It may give him a sleepless night. He will find it as sure a precursor of his fate as Openshaw did before him."

"And who is this Captain Calhoun?"

"The leader of the gang. I shall have the others, but he first."

"How did you trace it, then?"

He took a large sheet of paper from his pocket, all covered with dates and names.

"I have spent the whole day," said he, "over Lloyd's registers and files of the old papers, following the future career of every vessel which touched at Pondicherry in January and February in '83. There were thirty-six ships of fair tonnage which were reported there during those months. Of these, one, the 'Lone Star,' instantly attracted my attention, since, although it was reported as having cleared from London, the name is that which is given to one of the states of the Union."

"Texas, I think."

"I was not and am not sure which; but I knew that the ship must have an American origin."

"What then?"

"I searched the Dundee records, and when I found that the barque 'Lone Star' was there in January, '85, my suspicion became a certainty. I then inquired as to the vessels which lay at present in the port of London."

"Yes?"

"The 'Lone Star' had arrived here last week. I went down to the Albert Dock and found that she had been taken down the river by the early tide this morning, homeward bound to Savannah. I wired to Gravesend and learned that she had passed some time ago, and as the wind is easterly I have no doubt that she is now past the Goodwins and not very far from the Isle of Wight."

"What will you do, then?"

"Oh, I have my hand upon him. He and the two mates, are as I learn, the only native-born Americans in the ship. The others are Finns and Germans. I know, also, that they were all three away from the ship last night. I had it from the stevedore who has been loading their cargo. By the time that their sailing-ship reaches Savannah the mail-boat will have carried this letter, and the cable will have informed the police of Savannah that these three gentlemen are badly wanted here upon a charge of murder."

There is ever a flaw, however, in the best laid of human plans, and the murderers of John Openshaw were never to receive the orange pips which would show them that another, as cunning and as resolute as themselves, was upon their track. Very long and very severe were the equinoctial gales that year. We waited long for news of the "Lone Star" of Savannah, but none ever reached us. We did at last hear that somewhere far out in the Atlantic a shattered stern-post of a boat was seen swinging in the trough of a wave, with the letters "L. S." carved upon it, and that is all which we shall ever know of the fate of the "Lone Star."

"Let's take some of the pleading out of your plea bargain."

Lightning Source UK Ltd.
Milton Keynes UK
UKHW01f0113170518
322722UK00001B/96/P

9 781434 442079